Acting Edition

Birthday Club

by Phil Olson

‖ SAMUEL FRENCH ‖

No one shall make any changes in this title(s) for the purpose of production. No part of this book may be reproduced, stored in a retrieval system, scanned, uploaded, or transmitted in any form, by any means, now known or yet to be invented, including mechanical, electronic, digital, photocopying, recording, videotaping, or otherwise, without the prior written permission of the publisher. No one shall share this title(s), or any part of this title(s), through any social media or file hosting websites.

For all inquiries regarding motion picture, television, online/digital and other media rights, please contact Concord Theatricals Corp.

MUSIC AND THIRD-PARTY MATERIALS USE NOTE

Licensees are solely responsible for obtaining formal written permission from copyright owners to use copyrighted music and/or other copyrighted third-party materials (e.g., artworks, logos) in the performance of this play and are strongly cautioned to do so. If no such permission is obtained by the licensee, then the licensee must use only original music and materials that the licensee owns and controls. Licensees are solely responsible and liable for clearances of all third-party copyrighted materials, including without limitation music, and shall indemnify the copyright owners of the play(s) and their licensing agent, Concord Theatricals Corp., against any costs, expenses, losses and liabilities arising from the use of such copyrighted third-party materials by licensees. For music, please contact the appropriate music licensing authority in your territory for the rights to any incidental music.

IMPORTANT BILLING AND CREDIT REQUIREMENTS

If you have obtained performance rights to this title, please refer to your licensing agreement for important billing and credit requirements.

BIRTHDAY CLUB was first produced in Central Virginia by Persimmon Tree Players and Victory Hall Players in association with Scottsville's Center for the Arts and the Natural Environment, with virtual performances in March 2021. The producer was Tom Green, the directors were Courtney Walker and Kristin Freshwater, with technical direction by Tom Green, and sound by Mike Montgomery. The cast, in order of appearance, was as follows:

CHERYL. . . . . Mandy Shuker

EMILY. . . . . Emily Kinkead

ABBIE. . . . . .Jennifer LaFleur

KATHY . . . . Kelly Kroese

SARAH. . . . . Victoria Byler

BIRTHDAY CLUB was subsequently produced by the Mighty Richland Players Dessert Theater in Orangeville, Illinois in April 2021. The director was Kim McIver, the stage manager was Andy McIver, the set designer was Paula Fulton, and the lights and sound/tech crew were by Sue Wichman. The cast, in order of appearance, was as follows:

CHERYL. . . . . Terrie Miller

EMILY. . . . . .Sandy Sweitzer

ABBIE. . . . . Paula Fulton

KATHY . . . . .Amy Jo Beightol

SARAH. . . . . Keisha Leehan

BIRTHDAY CLUB is a winner in four playwriting competitions, including the Austin Film Festival Stage Play Competition, the Writer's Digest Stage Play Competition, the ScreenCraft Stage Play Competition, and the Mixing It Up Productions Playwright's Contest. The play had twenty-five Zoom readings in theatres around the US and Canada from March 2020 to February 2021.

CHARACTERS

CHERYL – (fifty) Married, successful business owner, anal-retentive, control issues. Marriage is strained. Stay-at-home husband.

EMILY – (forties) High school teacher. Divorced twice. Prolific Tinder dater. Has had lots of "work done."

ABBIE – (thirties) Married. Stay-at-home wife. Easy life. Nice big house, pool, boat.

KATHY – (forty) Works in "law enforcement." Married, four kids. Very tough.

SARAH – (twenties) Works for Cheryl. Member of the very strict "Heemish" religion. Wholesome, innocent, naive of all worldly things.

SETTING

Cheryl's living room

TIME

Present Day

ACT ONE

Scene One: Kathy's birthday.

Scene Two: Abbie's birthday. One month later.

Scene Three: Cheryl's birthday. A few months later.

ACT TWO

Scene One: Still Cheryl's birthday. Thirty seconds later.

Scene Two: Sarah's birthday. A few months later.

Scene Three: Emily's birthday. A few months later.

FOREWORD

I dedicate *Birthday Club* to Nancy Howland. I was the designated driver and observer of her Birthday Club for several years. Nancy has a close-knit group of loyal friends, with different personalities and backgrounds, who get together to celebrate, commiserate, and support each other while partaking in a glass or four of wine.

It was extremely entertaining and often times hysterical to be the "fly on the wall" and hear the candid conversations between these accomplished women. It was so entertaining that I asked Nancy if it would be okay to write a play about it, and with her permission and blessing, I wrote *Birthday Club*. Thank you, Nancy.

Phil Olson

Visit *PhilOlson.com* for more info about Phil's other plays and musicals.

ACT ONE

Scene One

(The setting is Cheryl's living room, nicely appointed, with a front door center stage right, a door to the kitchen upstage left, and an opening that leads to the den, bedrooms, and bathrooms, upstage center. In the living room is a couch, coffee table, two easy chairs, a dining table with four chairs around it, and a bar, downstage left, with wine bottles, glasses, and a fancy glass bottle filled with vodka, with a glass stopper [the kind of bottle that doesn't have any markings indicating it's vodka].)

(On the dining table is a fake birthday cake with unlit candles on it. On a coffee table in front of the couch is a bowl of crackers and a stack of coasters, napkins, and a martini shaker. Seated are **CHERYL, ABBIE, KATHY,** *and* **EMILY,** *all with a glass of wine. It's* **KATHY***'s birthday and she is very pregnant.* **CHERYL, EMILY,** *and* **ABBIE** *start singing "Happy Birthday.")*

CHERYL, EMILY & ABBIE. *(Singing to* **KATHY.***)*
HAPPY BIRTHDAY TO YOU,
HAPPY BIRTHDAY TO –

KATHY. Okay, that's enough. Let's drink.

CHERYL. Get 'em up, girls.

(The **WOMEN** *raise their wine glasses.)*

EMILY. To Kathy.

CHERYL, EMILY, ABBIE & KATHY. Birthday Club!

> *(They all take a drink, then put their glasses down on the coffee table.)*

CHERYL. Coasters!

> *(***CHERYL*** *passes out coasters to everyone. They put their glasses on the coasters.)*

ABBIE. *(Emotional.)* Can I just say that I am so grateful to be part of this group.

You have all been so kind to me when I really needed a friend –

KATHY. Yeah, great, fine. Less talking, more drinking.

> *(***KATHY*** *takes a drink.)*

CHERYL. Kathy.

KATHY. What? We *all* feel that way. It's *my* birthday. No sentiment.

> *(There's a knock at the door.)*

CHERYL. That must be Sarah.

EMILY. Is she the new member?

ABBIE. "Prospective" member.

KATHY. She's late.

> *(***CHERYL*** *heads over to answer the door.)*

ABBIE. How do you know her, again?

CHERYL. She works for me. She's a genius with numbers. I'm trying to groom her to be a manager but she's a little old-fashioned. I need your help to...bring her into the present.

(Another knock at the door.)

KATHY. Did you do a background check on her? Fingerprints?

*(**CHERYL** opens the door.)*

CHERYL. You made it.

SARAH. Sorry, I'm late. I got lost.

CHERYL. Oh, that's okay, it's your first time.

KATHY. First rule of Birthday Club, never be late.

EMILY. I thought it was, never talk about Birthday Club.

ABBIE. That's rule number three.

CHERYL. Everyone, this is Sarah.

EMILY, ABBIE & KATHY. Hi, Sarah.

SARAH. Hi.

CHERYL. This is Emily, Kathy and Abbie.

SARAH. Who's the birthday girl?

KATHY. *(Raises her hand.)* Present.

SARAH. Happy birthday. How old are you?

KATHY. Whoa, whoa, whoa!

EMILY. What the what?!

CHERYL. Rule number two: "Never discuss age at Birthday Club."

SARAH. Oh, I'm sorry.

KATHY. Jeez.

ABBIE. It's okay. She didn't know.

*(**KATHY** sets her wine down and heads to the bar.)*

KATHY. Can I get you a drink? We have wine, vodka...

SARAH. Oh, thanks, how about just a glass of water. I brought my own orange flavoring.

KATHY. Is she serious? Are you serious?

SARAH. Yeah, I can't drink alcohol.

KATHY. Why is she here?

CHERYL. For a different perspective. Now, be nice.

ABBIE. You've never had alcohol?

SARAH. No. It's not allowed in the Heemish religion.

EMILY. "Heemish"?

KATHY. What the hell is the Heemish religion?

SARAH. Oh, we're not allowed to swear. Or listen to swear words.

KATHY. Hell's not a swear word. It's in the Bible. Here's a swear word for you, I'll spell it, F. U. –

CHERYL. *(Cuts her off.)* Kathy!

SARAH. It's a very strict religion. Almost as strict as the Amish, except we can use toasters.

ABBIE. Is she joking? I can't tell.

SARAH. Oh, no, they don't allow us to joke.

EMILY. That seems like a joke.

KATHY. So, you don't know what alcohol tastes like?

SARAH. No.

KATHY. I'll get you some water.

(*Whispers to* CHERYL.) I don't trust her.

(KATHY *pours* SARAH *a glass of water. She spills some.*)

Oh, shoot, I spilled.

CHERYL, EMILY & ABBIE. Napkin!

(**KATHY** *grabs a napkin and wipes up the spill.*)

KATHY. Rule number six: "Never spill at Birthday Club."

EMILY. Cheryl is a little...particular.

CHERYL. A clean house is a happy house.

SARAH. Amen.

(*She sees a birthday cake on the table.*)

Oh, the cake looks good. What kind is it?

ABBIE. Oh, that's fake. We don't eat cake at Birthday Club.

EMILY. Too many calories.

ABBIE. We just look at it.

EMILY. We eat cupcakes. They're smaller.

CHERYL. So we eat, like, six of 'em.

ABBIE. *(To **SARAH**.)* Can I ask, if you can't drink or joke in the Heemish religion, what are you allowed to do?

SARAH. Oh, well, we can get married and have babies. And if you're a woman, you can work until you have children.

EMILY. Wow.

ABBIE. That seems very...1800s.

(**KATHY** *comes back with the glass of water. She holds the glass at the very bottom to not get fingerprints on the upper part of the glass. She hands it to **SARAH**.*)

KATHY. Here you go.

(**SARAH** *takes the glass.*)

Oh, you know what, that glass is dirty. I'll get another one.

(**KATHY** *takes the glass from* **SARAH**, *holding it, again, at the very bottom. She heads back to the bar.*)

SARAH. Oh, no, you don't have to wait on me. I can get it.

KATHY. Okay.

(**SARAH** *goes to the bar.*)

SARAH. So, does everybody pool together to get a present, or...

CHERYL. No presents at Birthday Club.

(*At the bar,* **KATHY** *takes out a makeup brush and brushes the side of* **SARAH**'s *glass.*)

SARAH. What are you doing?

KATHY. Cleaning.

(**SARAH** *picks up the crystal vodka bottle and opens the top, ready to pour in a clean glass.*)

(*Not noticing what* **SARAH** *is doing,* **CHERYL** *grabs her cell phone to take a photo of* **ABBIE** *and* **EMILY**.)

CHERYL. Smile.

(**EMILY** *and* **ABBIE** *make faces,* **CHERYL** *takes the photo.*)

Perfect.

(**CHERYL** *looks at the photo, then shows it to* **EMILY** *and* **ABBIE**.)

SARAH. (*Re: the vodka bottle.*) Fancy water bottle.

KATHY. (*To* **SARAH**, *warning her.*) Oh, no, that's not...

(**SARAH** *fills a glass with vodka,* **KATHY** *looks to see the others aren't looking.*)

SARAH. Not what?

KATHY. Nothin'.

SARAH. So, when is your baby due?

(**SARAH** *puts orange flavor in her "water."*)

KATHY. What baby?

SARAH. Aren't you…?

(*She points to* **KATHY**'s *stomach.*)

Oh, I am so sorry. I'm so embarrassed.

KATHY. *(Looking at her stomach.)* Whoa! Where'd this come from?

SARAH. *(Uncertain.)* She's…joking, right?

EMILY. Yeah. Kathy does that sometimes.

KATHY. *(To* **SARAH**.*)* Just a heads up, I can be a little abrasive sometimes.

CHERYL. *(Sarcastic.)* Noooooooooooooo.

KATHY. But it's all done with affection. I love these bitches –

(*Corrects herself for* **SARAH**.*)* Ladies. I have their backs, and I'd do anything for 'em.

SARAH. That's nice.

ABBIE. I thought you said no sentiment.

KATHY. It's *my* birthday.

SARAH. *(Takes a drink.)* Oh, this tastes funny. What kind of water is this?

KATHY. Vitamin water. Lots of nutrients.

(*With her cell phone,* **KATHY** *takes a picture of the glass with fingerprints, texts the photo to someone.*)

(**SARAH** *goes back and sits down.*)

ABBIE. *(To* **KATHY.***)* When are you due, in four weeks?

KATHY. Four more glorious weeks of swollen ankles, heartburn and constant peeing, followed by twenty pounds I'll never lose.

> (**KATHY** *goes back and sits. She picks up her wine glass.*)

SARAH. I can't wait to have children. I'm sure you're looking forward to it.

KATHY. Not at all. This is my fourth. Purely an accident. I didn't even think I could have kids anymore.

SARAH. Just curious, is alcohol good for the baby?

KATHY. Oh, yeah, my doctor said it was okay to have a glass of wine.

CHERYL. When did he tell you that? 1952?

EMILY. My doctor said the same thing, especially in the third trimester.

KATHY. Hey, my mom drank through her entire pregnancy with me and I turned out just fine.

> (**EMILY, CHERYL,** *and* **ABBIE** *break out laughing.* **SARAH** *laughs, following the others.*)

SARAH. That's crazy.

ABBIE. Uh-oh.

KATHY. *(Very serious.)* Pregnant woman are not "crazy." We have superpowers derived from our baby-making skills, that can be misinterpreted.

SARAH. Oh, of course. I'm sorry, I didn't mean anything by it.

CHERYL. Okay, let's go over a few more Birthday Club rules.

SARAH. You have a lot of rules.

KATHY. Without rules, we'd have chaos. Do you want chaos?

SARAH. Oh, no, I'm happy to follow any rules you have. I really wanna be in your club. I don't have many friends.

KATHY. Hmm, surprising.

CHERYL. We have eight rules. To add a new rule, you make a motion to do so, then we vote on the new rule with a majority required to ratify it.

SARAH. Got it.

(SARAH takes another drink.)

CHERYL. Okay, so we meet whenever somebody has a birthday. Pretty simple. We always meet at my house.

SARAH. Sounds good. Thanks for letting me be part of your group.

KATHY. Oooh, yeah, about that…you're not actually a member of the club until you're formally initiated.

SARAH. Oh, sure, okay.

KATHY. We're very selective.

ABBIE. There's a three-year waiting list to get in.

EMILY. The thing is, we do important work here. Lots of people wanna be members.

CHERYL. Oftentimes, we make life-or-death decisions.

EMILY. Like whether to go with vodka or wine.

SARAH. Wow. Okay, so, how do I become a member?

(SARAH takes another drink.)

CHERYL. Well, you first need to learn our history. Abbie?

ABBIE. Sure. We started Birthday Club five years ago when a friend of ours, Jennifer, was diagnosed with cancer.

SARAH. Oh, no.

EMILY. Birthday Club helped Jennifer get through some
pretty tough times.

SARAH. Oh, I'm so sorry. How is she doing?

KATHY. She's dead.

CHERYL. Kathy.

KATHY. Well, she is. Which brings up rule number four:
"Never miss Birthday Club for any reason. Reschedule
any work conflicts, family vacations, weddings,
funerals, illnesses or pandemics."

CHERYL. The bottom line is, the only valid reason to miss
Birthday Club is if you are dead.

EMILY. And that excuse has a caveat.

(**EMILY** *picks up the martini shaker.*)

Say hi to Jennifer.

SARAH. That's Jennifer?! In the...?!

KATHY. Martini shaker. It's what she wanted.

SARAH. That is so...sad.

(**SARAH** *takes another drink.*)

KATHY. Yeah, very sad. Lots of tears. That's why you're
here. We had an opening.

(*To* **CHERYL**.) Did you not tell her anything?

CHERYL. I've been getting a little forgetful, lately. Which
reminds me, I need to take my meds.

(**CHERYL** *takes out a bottle and pops a couple
pills, drinks, and washes it down with wine.*)

EMILY, KATHY & ABBIE. *(Singing to "If You're Happy and You Know It.")*
IF YOU'RE HAPPY AND YOU KNOW IT,
IT'S YOUR MEDS.

*(**KATHY, ABBIE,** and **EMILY** clap twice.)*

SARAH. Do those help with your memory?

KATHY. She has the menopause.

EMILY. "The" menopause. Isn't it just, "menopause"?

KATHY. Not what *she* has.

CHERYL. My brain keeps hitting the delete button.

SARAH. Oh, is that what the menopause does?

CHERYL. That and the sleep deprivation, weight gain, cellulite and depression. Oh, and I pee when I sneeze.

KATHY. Doesn't everyone?

CHERYL. And, oh, yeah, I'm growing a mustache.

KATHY. Hydrogen peroxide. Without it, I'd be Wolf Man.

ABBIE. *(To **CHERYL.**)* How are your mood swings?

CHERYL. Oh, I don't have mood swings. I have the whole friggin' playground.

KATHY. Something else to look forward to.

CHERYL. Okay, where were we? Oh, yeah, cancer. So when Jennifer was diagnosed, we started Birthday Club as kind of a support group.

EMILY. We wanted it to be a fun, happy time, when we could forget life's struggles for a few hours.

KATHY. Because life sucks.

CHERYL. Kathy.

ABBIE. We wanted this to be a place where there were no filters, where we could talk about anything without being judged, out loud.

EMILY. And drink.

KATHY. Which we are not doing enough of.

SARAH. How did you all meet?

(**SARAH** *takes another drink.*)

ABBIE. We met at yoga.

KATHY. That's when we were actually going to yoga.

EMILY. Some of us still go.

SARAH. What do you all do? I mean, I know what Cheryl does, she runs a successful CPA firm. And she's a great boss. Very inspiring.

KATHY. Yeah, kissing ass will not get you points.

CHERYL. Oh, it'll get you *some* points.

EMILY. I'm a teacher at Lincoln High.

ABBIE. *(Re:* **EMILY.***)* She's getting her PhD in education.

SARAH. Wow.

KATHY. I work for a branch in law enforcement that requires a specific set of skills. That's all I can say.

SARAH. That can mean a lot of things.

KATHY. And it does.

(*She puts her index and middle fingers to her eyes, then points to* **SARAH** *à la* Meet the Parents, *i.e.* "*I'm watching you.*")

ABBIE. I'm a homemaker.

SARAH. Oh, congratulations.

KATHY. She has a big house, swimming pool, tennis court.

SARAH. Wow.

CHERYL. And she has four pocket doors.

SARAH. Oh, I love pocket doors.

EMILY. Country club, no kids. She has a nice life.

ABBIE. It's pretty sweet.

SARAH. You're all so impressive.

ABBIE. *(Re:* **SARAH***.)* I like her.

> **(SARAH** *takes another drink. She's a little tipsy.)*

SARAH. This is tasty. Has a little bite to it.

EMILY. Cheryl, where's your husband tonight?

CHERYL. Dave is watching the game over at Gary's.

EMILY. How's his book coming?

CHERYL. *(Dismissive.)* His book? Oh, I don't know. He says he's almost done with it. He's only been writing it for, like, five years.

SARAH. So, Dave writes books for a living?

CHERYL. "For a living"?

> *(Laughs.)*

That's funny.

ABBIE. Well, he did take care of the kids so you could work.

CHERYL. Yeah, that's true. He was a stay-at-home dad, and he was good at that. But now that the kids have been in college for a few years, he just stays at home and "writes."

SARAH. Does he have anything published?

CHERYL. *(Laughs.)* "Published."

(SARAH takes another drink.)

SARAH. Where did you get this water?

KATHY. The water store.

EMILY. So, Sarah, do you have any questions for us?

SARAH. Do you ever let men join the club?

(Everyone looks at her for a few beats. Then:)

KATHY. Please leave.

CHERYL. No men allowed in Birthday Club.

SARAH. Oh, no, I'm sorry. My mistake. It won't happen again. I promise.

CHERYL. Okay, let's get down to business. Who's first?

EMILY. I broke up with Tyler.

ABBIE. Is that the guy with the Porsche?

EMILY. No, that was Jason. Tyler has a Mercedes.

ABBIE. What happened?

EMILY. He didn't like my new boobs, and I was like, well, I didn't get 'em for *you*, I got 'em for *me*! Gah!

KATHY. What a jerk.

EMILY. Sarah, you wanna feel 'em?

SARAH. Oh, my. Umm, no...thank you, though...for the offer.

ABBIE. *(To* **EMILY.***)* He doesn't deserve you.

EMILY. That's what *I* said. So, I met another guy on Tinder.

SARAH. What's Tinder?

KATHY. Oh, good Lord.

EMILY. It's a dating website.

SARAH. Oh.

EMILY. You've never been on a dating site?

SARAH. Oh, no, we're not allowed to use the internet. Besides, I'm engaged. To my high school sweetheart.

EMILY. What high school?

SARAH. Oh, we were homeschooled. There were two in our class. I was class president.

ABBIE. Of a two-person class?

SARAH. I know. It was a pretty big honor.

KATHY. Is that weird for anyone else?

SARAH. He was the first guy I ever went out with.

EMILY. So, you've only been with one man?

SARAH. Yes, I've only dated one man.

(She takes another drink.)

KATHY. But you've *been* with other men.

SARAH. What do you mean, "been with"?

KATHY. Is this happening? Is this real?

ABBIE. She means, have you ever had "relations" with another man.

SARAH. Oh, I see. No, no I've never had relations with any man. I'm saving myself for marriage.

EMILY. Is it not allowed?

SARAH. As Bathaldafor said to Mefluzala, "Tempt ye not, for impure waters taste of curdled goat cheese."

KATHY. Am I being punked?

(Looking around.) Is there a hidden camera somewhere?

CHERYL. Kathy, no judgments.

ABBIE. So, Sarah, how many years have you been going out with your fiancé?

SARAH. With Mordecai? Oh, umm, seven years.

ABBIE. "Mordecai"?

EMILY. Okay, you've been going out for seven years and you haven't even...

KATHY. How is that even possible?

SARAH. It's what we follow.

CHERYL. Do you ever bend the rules?

SARAH. I bent the rules coming here.

CHERYL. How so?

SARAH. Well, Mordecai was apprehensive about letting me come to Birthday Club.

KATHY. "Letting you"? Where's my gun?

(**SARAH** *takes a drink. She's getting more tipsy.*)

SARAH. He was nervous that you might be a bad influence on me by playing a PG-rated movie, or doing karaoke.

EMILY. That would be horrible... It actually would.

(*Grimaces.*) "Karaoke."

SARAH. But because we're at my boss's house, he thought it might help me at work, so he approved.

KATHY. "He approved"? So disturbing.

SARAH. I'm getting a little lightheaded.

ABBIE. Have a cracker.

(**SARAH** *grabs a cracker and holds on to it.*)

KATHY. What would happen if you drank alcohol and Mordecai found out?

SARAH. Oh, he would never talk to me again. It would be over. But that wouldn't happen because I would never drink alcohol.

(She takes another drink.)

This is so good.

(She eats the cracker.)

Yum, yum, yum, yum, yum.

KATHY. Well, we try not to encourage bad behavior.

(She takes out her cell phone.)

Sorry, I gotta get this.

(Into the phone.) Yeah?... What?! No, I already told you, no... If you ask me again, I will take you into the woods and leave you for the wolves to eat. And no one will ever find you, because you will be eaten by wolves.

(She hangs up.)

Sorry.

SARAH. Who was that?

KATHY. My daughter... She wants a new tricycle.

SARAH. *(Processing that.)* So...how am I doing so far?

KATHY. Well, you passed the credit report.

SARAH. You ran a credit report?

ABBIE. And since you've been working for Cheryl for over a year, she's spoken very highly of you.

SARAH. *(To* **CHERYL.***)* Thank you.

EMILY. So, Sarah, are you in acceptance of our rules so far?

SARAH. Does anyone say "no"?

ABBIE. Not yet.

KATHY. We don't choose people who might say no.

CHERYL. But don't worry, saying no will not reflect poorly on your continued employment with me.

(**CHERYL** *laughs.*)

SARAH. Wait, does that mean that it will?

CHERYL. No. Yes.

(*She laughs.*)

You're funny.

SARAH. That doesn't answer whether it, umm –

KATHY. Okay, just a few more things; when we all first joined, we went around and told something about ourselves that was very personal, a secret that no one else knows, something that would be very damaging if it ever got out.

SARAH. I'm sorry, what?

EMILY. We just want to make sure you're committed to Birthday Club.

SARAH. Are you serious?

ABBIE. Very serious. When you join the club, you're making a commitment to everyone here that you'll abide by our secrecy policy. We just wanna insure that.

SARAH. Do I get to know *your* secrets?

KATHY. Absolutely.

SARAH. Okay...

(*Thinks.*)

Well, I went on a Rogastragger a few years ago.

ABBIE. What's a rogastragger –

SARAH. It's the Heemish version of Rumspringa.

CHERYL. It's where they leave the family, go to the city, and sow their wild oats for a few months.

SARAH. And I met a guy, not my fiancé.

KATHY. Did you...

('70s porn music-esque.) Brown chicken, brown cow.

SARAH. I don't know what that is, but...we kissed. On the cheek, but still.

EMILY. That's it?

SARAH. If Mordecai ever found out, he'd never marry me. And I would be sent to the disgrace room for a week.

ABBIE. I've been there.

SARAH. It would be the worst. I would never live it down.

EMILY. I gotta say, that's pretty risky telling us that.

SARAH. I know. It could destroy me.

ABBIE. Well, thanks for your trust.

SARAH. Sure. Okay, now tell me *your* secrets.

KATHY. Yeah, no, we don't do that. We were just messing with you. I'm surprised you went along with it. Kudos.

*(**SARAH** is very tipsy now.)*

SARAH. Wow. I did *not* see that coming.

KATHY. And now you're tougher for it. You gotta be able to take anything that life throws at you. And we prepare you for that. You're welcome.

SARAH. So...did I pass?

KATHY. One more thing. Pop quiz: you're stranded on a desert island with a man and a woman. Do you kill the man or kill the woman?

SARAH. Umm...neither?

KATHY. Wrong. You kill the man. The man will just create friction between the two women, probably end up sleeping with both of 'em, pitting them against each other, causing chaos.

KATHY. *(To* **EMILY.***)* Nobody ever gets that one right.

CHERYL. *(To* **SARAH.***)* That won't count against you.

ABBIE. Did you find anything, Kathy?

KATHY. I'll make the call.

> *(Hitting speed dial on her phone.)* Just a minute.

SARAH. "Find anything"?

KATHY. *(Into her phone.)* Did you run the prints?

SARAH. Run, what now?

KATHY. How about her social security number?

SARAH. What's going on?

KATHY. A little skirmish with her father and a neighbor over a broken buggy whip, but it was resolved.

SARAH. Who is she talking to?

KATHY. Otherwise, no criminal record, or social media presence. Great, thanks. I owe you.

> *(She hangs up.)*

> *(To the others.)* She's clean.

SARAH. What just happened?

CHERYL. Girls?

> *(They all nod to* **CHERYL.***)*

Congratulations. You're officially a member of Birthday Club.

> *(They all raise their glasses.)*

ALL. *(Except* **SARAH.***)* Birthday Club!

> *(***SARAH** *finishes her "orange water.")*

SARAH. *(Drunk.)* I just have to say that this is such an honor, and, I feel really funny.

CHERYL. *(To* KATHY.*)* Did you give her alcohol?

KATHY. No. She poured it herself.

SARAH. *(Drunk.)* Thank you so much. I've never been so happy in my entire –

(**SARAH** *passes out, drunk. After a few beats:)*

KATHY. We should probably get her to a hospital.

EMILY. Yeah.

(Blackout.)

Scene Two

> *(Abbie's birthday.* **CHERYL, SARAH, EMILY,**
> **KATHY,** *and* **ABBIE** *are in the living room.*
> **KATHY** *is still very pregnant. All but* **ABBIE**
> *sing the first line of "Happy Birthday.")*

ALL. *(Except* **ABBIE.)**

HAPPY BIRTHDAY TO –

KATHY. Okay, that's good. Let's drink.

> **(CHERYL, ABBIE, EMILY,** *and* **KATHY** *hold up*
> *wine glasses. A glass of "orange water" rests*
> *on the coffee table.)*

ALL. *(Except* **ABBIE.)** To Abbie.

ALL. Birthday Club!

> *(They all drink, except* **SARAH.)**

CHERYL. Coasters!

KATHY. *(Bothered by coasters.)* Yeah, yeah, yeah.

> *(They put their drinks on coasters.)*

EMILY. Sarah, why aren't you drinking?

SARAH. I don't drink.

KATHY. You didn't have a problem drinking last time.

SARAH. I didn't know it was alcohol.

KATHY. I tried to warn you.

SARAH. Did you?

KATHY. Hey, it was just vodka. Liquid potatoes.

SARAH. I'm sorry, but I'm afraid I won't be coming back
to Birthday Club after tonight. I just wanted to tell you
in person.

CHERYL. Why not?

SARAH. Well, I hate to say it, but I think you all might be a bad influence on me.

ABBIE. Why would you think that?

SARAH. Well, I guess because the last time I was here I had to go to the hospital and have my stomach pumped so I wouldn't die from alcohol poisoning.

KATHY. Welcome to the club.

SARAH. I told Mordecai I had food poisoning. I lied. If he ever found out the truth, he would place a pox on me.

ABBIE. What, like a metaphorical pox?

SARAH. No, a real pox, with blisters.

ABBIE. Ewe.

EMILY. I'm sorry but you can't quit.

KATHY. Yeah, we kind of like you.

SARAH. You don't understand. Alcohol is forbidden. I lied to Mordecai. I committed two sins. You know how many public shamings I'd have to attend if they found out?

CHERYL. Well, don't they forgive you?

SARAH. Yes, but last time I had to spend six days in the church silo thrashing my knuckles.

EMILY. So many things wrong with that.

CHERYL. So, were you forgiven?

SARAH. At the time, but I couldn't churn butter for two days.

EMILY. I hate when that happens.

SARAH. I'm gonna tell Mordecai the truth, and that I'm gonna quit Birthday Club.

KATHY. I know how we can solve this. Tell him you quit Birthday Club, then don't.

(**ABBIE** *takes a drink.*)

SARAH. But that would be lying. Again.

KATHY. And?...

SARAH. If I'm caught, he'll leave me, and I'll be banished from the summer leech breeding.

ABBIE. That's a thing?

KATHY. Don't tell him.

SARAH. But *I* would know.

KATHY. Oh, no. She's got morals. Have some orange water and think about it.

(*Hands her "orange water."*)

SARAH. Thanks.

(*Takes a drink.*)

This is vodka!

KATHY. Just cradle it.

(**SARAH** *sets down the vodka.*)

EMILY. Are you sure Mordecai is right for you?

SARAH. What do you mean?

EMILY. Well, it seems like you're sacrificing a lot for someone you may not be compatible with, you know, romantically.

SARAH. What do you mean, "compatible"?

ABBIE. Do you "work well" together, you know, in "that way."

EMILY. Did your homeschooling ever teach you sex education? I mean, you know where everything goes, right?

SARAH. We called it "Suppression Education," and, yes, I know all the terms; my "naughty place," my "evil twins," my "exit only."

CHERYL. *(Processes that.)* Okay, we're not gonna solve this right now. Let's put a pin in Sarah's issue, and we'll come back to it.

SARAH. Maybe I should just leave.

KATHY. What you should do is stay and listen to those of us who have experience with men.

ABBIE. *You* are the boss of *you.*

CHERYL. You don't report to Mordecai. You need to train him just like I've trained my husband.

EMILY. Where is Dave tonight?

CHERYL. He's at the library, writing his "great new novel."

ABBIE. She's a little skeptical.

CHERYL. If you're saying that I don't think he has the drive or ability to finish it, you'd be correct.

SARAH. Maybe he just needs some encouragement.

I mean, you're so inspirational to me, maybe you can share that inspiration with your husband.

CHERYL. Well, I tried to inspire him to go back to engineering, but he decided to write a book instead.

SARAH. What's his book about?

CHERYL. Oh, it's a murder mystery about a guy who kills his controlling wife.

KATHY. So, it's based on a true story.

CHERYL. Oh, I get it. I'm the controlling wife.

EMILY. Well, you are the Type-A breadwinner in the family. I mean, it's understandable.

CHERYL. I have a lot of responsibilities.

(**CHERYL** *picks up a magazine and starts fanning herself.*)

ABBIE. You okay?

CHERYL. Oh, my gosh, I'm burning up. Is it hot in here?

EMILY. It's sixty-five degrees.

ABBIE. You're having a hot flash.

CHERYL. I don't have hot flashes. I have power surges.

KATHY. Work through it.

SARAH. A hot flash?

KATHY. Yeah, you feel like you're on fire.

CHERYL. Last night I evaporated the water in my bathtub.

SARAH. How?

ABBIE. It's the menopause. It makes your body do crazy things.

CHERYL. I wouldn't mind the hot flashes as much if they just burned a little fat off my thighs.

SARAH. It sounds horrible.

CHERYL. Actually, menopause isn't really that bad...said no woman, ever.

KATHY. Fortunately, it doesn't happen till you get old.

CHERYL. Thank you. Okay, let's get to business. Abbie?

ABBIE. Well, it was a busy week, I had a nice lunch at the club, I finished my book, bought a new dress at Nordstroms, my husband left me, I went to a matinee –

EMILY. – Whoa, whoa, whoa, pump the brakes, there. Your husband left you?

ABBIE. *(Crying.)* Yes.

CHERYL. Why didn't you lead with that?

ABBIE. *(Emotional.)* I just try to shut it down, bottle it up, deny my feelings. He was everything to me. And now, I'm dead inside. My life is over.

SARAH. Let's pray.

> (**SARAH** *folds her hands, looks around, no one wants to pray,* **ABBIE** *takes a drink.)*

Amen.

KATHY. We need to take him down. Destroy him. Where is he?

ABBIE. I still love him.

KATHY. She's been programmed.

CHERYL. Do you love *him,* or do you love the financial security he provides?

ABBIE. *(Emotional.)* Isn't it the same thing?

EMILY. Okay, we need to clear your mind, get you on Tinder. Get right back up in the saddle.

SARAH. What do you mean by "saddle"?

EMILY. Abbie needs a little banana in her fruit salad.

SARAH. Oh. My uncle grows bananas.

ABBIE. Men are horrible.

CHERYL. What happened?

ABBIE. He left me for a fetus.

SARAH. A fetus?

ABBIE. She's like twelve years old.

SARAH. I thought the legal age was fourteen.

EMILY. In what century?

ABBIE. She's not literally twelve. She's a nursing student.

SARAH. I'm so sorry.

ABBIE. I supported him.

KATHY. Wait, you did?

ABBIE. Emotionally.

CHERYL. What are you gonna do?

ABBIE. *(Emotional.)* I don't know. I might have to go back to work. I haven't worked since I got married. Who's gonna hire me?

CHERYL. You can come work for me.

EMILY. Best thing for you to do right now is to feed that kitty.

SARAH. *(To* ABBIE.*)* Oh, do you have a cat?

ABBIE. Who's gonna want my kitty? I wear Spanx!

SARAH. I'll take your kitty. I live on a farm. Kitties love mice.

EMILY. Lots of guys like women who wear Spanx.

KATHY. Yeah, no they don't.

EMILY. I know, I'm just trying to make her feel better.

ABBIE. Oh, crap, I'm gonna have to go on a diet.

KATHY. I can help with that. Just avoid things that make you fat, like scales, mirrors and photographs.

ABBIE. Maybe he'll come back. Maybe he'll leave the hot, young, nursing student.

KATHY. Yeah, and maybe monkeys will fly outta your butt.

EMILY. It's competitive out there. The pressure to look young and in shape.

ABBIE. That's not encouraging.

EMILY. Next week I'm having placenta injections in my face. Makes you look ten years younger.

(To **ABBIE.***)* You want me to hook you up with my Placent-ologist?

SARAH. Emily, you're so beautiful. You don't need those things to make you look prettier. And do you really wanna be with someone that thinks you do?

EMILY. Oh, you're so sweet.

ABBIE. What about me?

SARAH. You?... You're beautiful in your own way.

ABBIE. *(Cries.)* Ohhh.

KATHY. Have more alcohol.

(**ABBIE** *takes a drink.)*

I know a guy who will kneecap him. You want me to call him?

ABBIE. I want him back.

KATHY. Why?!

ABBIE. I still love him.

CHERYL. You love the lifestyle.

ABBIE. *(Emotional.)* It's a nice lifestyle.

EMILY. It's a *very* nice lifestyle. But is it worth it?

ABBIE. I don't understand the question.

EMILY. Is he worth staying with just for all those nice things?

ABBIE. That seems like the same question.

CHERYL. He cheated on you.

ABBIE. I can forgive him. Pretend it never happened.

ABBIE. *(To* KATHY.*)* Would you wanna know if your husband cheated on you if it had no impact on your relationship?

KATHY. Hell, yeah.

EMILY. Obviously, you don't love him.

ABBIE. *(Emotional.)* We have a seventy-foot sailboat!

KATHY. Why haven't *I* been on it?!... Okay, that's it, your time is up.

(*To* SARAH.*)* Next. Sarah?

SARAH. *(Taken offguard.)* Oh, umm, Emily, are you married?

EMILY. Divorced twice, daughter, a senior in high school, looking at colleges. She just came out last week.

KATHY. Finally.

SARAH. Where was she?

EMILY. In the closet.

SARAH. What was she doing in there?

EMILY. She's gay.

SARAH. Oh... We have a program for that.

KATHY. *(To* CHERYL, *re:* SARAH.*)* Did she just say that?

CHERYL. We'll get there.

ABBIE. Hello! We have a situation here.

(**ABBIE** *gestures to herself.*)

EMILY. *(To* ABBIE.*)* What you need is a man.

CHERYL. No, you don't.

EMILY. You need to get on Tinder and swipe right on every guy you see.

CHERYL. You don't need a man.

SARAH. Do you use Tinder a lot?

EMILY. I'm a frequent flyer. I get points.

KATHY. She dates a lot of underwear models with nice cars.

SARAH. Well, as long as they're intellectually stimulating.

EMILY. *(Laughs.)* "Intellectually." That's funny.

ABBIE. That's not her top priority.

EMILY. Hey, I know a couple guys that'll go out with anyone. But they're into stuff. Do you have a snorkel?

SARAH. Why would she need a snorkel –

ABBIE. You don't think I should be picky?

EMILY. No. Right now you need to get your oil changed.

SARAH. I use 10W-40.

KATHY. You drive a car?

SARAH. No. It's for my buggy wheels.

ABBIE. I think I'm just gonna drink myself to death.

(**ABBIE** *takes a drink.*)

KATHY. That would be irresponsible. Just drink yourself unconscious. Like Sarah.

CHERYL. Don't overdo it, Abbie. You know how you get.

EMILY. *(Looks out front window.)* Hold on a minute, what's this?

(**EMILY** *stands up and walks to the front of the stage, looking out. One by one the rest of them walk downstage, looking out.*)

KATHY. Holy crap.

CHERYL. That's my new neighbor.

SARAH. What's he doing?

KATHY. He's washing his car. Duh.

SARAH. Yeah, but why is he washing it so late and without a shirt?

(*Realizing.*) Oh, no, I shouldn't be looking at that.

(**SARAH** *looks away.*)

ABBIE. Why not?

SARAH. As Ezrakabash said to the Luddiframites, "Look not upon thy flesh, lest ye be smitten by the smiter."

KATHY. What does that even mean?

EMILY. Who cares? Just enjoy it.

ABBIE. He looks like a Chippendale dancer.

EMILY. Scrub a dub dub.

SARAH. Should I go out and tell him we can see him?

EMILY. Don't you dare!

CHERYL. He's looking this way.

(*They all drop to the floor, "out of sight" from the neighbor.*)

He didn't see us, did he?

EMILY. Does it matter?

CHERYL. Yes. I don't want him to think I'm a pervert.

EMILY. (*Pokes her head up, looks.*) Oh, my god, I could eat sushi off those abs.

(*Ducks down.*)

I think he saw me.

KATHY. Oh, I gotta sit down. Too much excitement.

(**KATHY** *goes back to the couch.* **EMILY** *stands up and looks out at car wash guy.*)

EMILY. He's very flexible.

CHERYL. Emily, get down.

EMILY. I bet he can do the splits.

CHERYL. Would you get down –

EMILY. Relax. He's not looking.

> *(They all stand up and look out, including* **SARAH.***)*

SARAH. Now, I'm gonna have to join the regret share circle and say ten Nebuchadnezzars. *(Pronounced "nebahkahnezzer.")*

ABBIE. Why?

SARAH. Looking at a shirtless man all sweaty and soapy and wet and...soapy.

EMILY. Writhing around in his little short shorts.

KATHY. He's not wearing short shorts.

EMILY. He's wearing 'em in my porn fantasy.

SARAH. They don't have men like that at our barn raisings.

EMILY. Men with smooth skin and bulging bulges.

(Yelling at him.) Over here!

CHERYL. Stop it!

ABBIE. He's looking.

> *(They all duck down again, except* **EMILY,** *who seductively dances for car wash guy.)*

CHERYL. What are you doing?!

EMILY. I learned this in pole dancing class.

CHERYL. Why?!

EMILY. Oh, he's going inside. Darn it.

> *(They all go back and sit down.* **ABBIE** *takes another drink. She's very tipsy.)*

CHERYL. That was embarrassing.

EMILY. Oh, hey, that reminds me, Sarah, are you gonna be here next time for Cheryl's birthday?

SARAH. I suppose. Why?

EMILY. Oh, I just wanted to give you something. So, Cheryl, is your neighbor available?

CHERYL. You wanna date my neighbor?

EMILY. Well, not me, I was thinking of Abbie. But now that you mention it.

ABBIE. How old is he?

CHERYL. I don't know, I think he's in his thirties.

EMILY. Perfect.

ABBIE. *(Very tipsy.)* I would have no idea what to do with a hot beefcake like that. But I'm willing to find out.

(She stands up.)

Who wants to go streaking?!

EMILY. I might if it was the 1970s.

CHERYL. Are you drunk?

ABBIE. Not enough. Let's get naked!

(**ABBIE** *runs out the door.)*

CHERYL. No, don't go out there.

(**ABBIE**'s *gone.)*

(Groans.) Ahh.

(They all get up and look out the window.)

SARAH. What is she doing?

EMILY. It looks like she's breakdancing.

CHERYL. We have got to limit the alcohol intake.

KATHY. Oh, her Spanx are coming off.

SARAH. *(Grimaces.)* Ohhh!

KATHY. And there they go.

EMILY. Why did she throw 'em in the street?

CHERYL. Abbie, come back in!

EMILY. Oh, she's peeing. She's peeing in the yard.

CHERYL. *(Yelling to* **ABBIE.***)* We have a bathroom!

SARAH. Oh, my gosh, should I go get her?

KATHY. Speaking of peeing, I'll be right back.

> (**KATHY** *walks into the hallway, holding her wine.)*

EMILY. *(Re:* **ABBIE.***)* She definitely needs some grooming down there.

KATHY. *(Offstage.)* Oh, look at that, my water broke.

CHERYL. Your what?!

KATHY. *(Coming back in the room, casually.)* My water just broke.

> *(She takes a drink.)*

SARAH. *(Going to* **KATHY.***)* Are you serious?! Your water broke?

> *(Looks down the hall.)*

Oh, my gosh, her water broke!

CHERYL. Get a towel.

KATHY. Clean up on aisle four.

SARAH. We gotta get her to a birthing pond!

KATHY. Relax, this ain't my first rodeo.

CHERYL. C'mon, let's go. They have a birthing pond at the hospital.

KATHY. Let me just finish this.

(She takes a final drink.)

SARAH. It's all over the place. Oh, my goodness, my head feels funny. It's like when I was six and my first cow gave birth, it was a breech, and it was so messy, and I passed out, and I feel like I'm gonna…down we go.

(She passes out.)

KATHY. Okay, let's get her up.

*(**EMILY** and **CHERYL** help lift up **SARAH** and start toward the front door with **KATHY** just as **ABBIE** comes back, drunk.)*

ABBIE. What did I miss?

EMILY. Kathy is having a baby right now, Sarah passed out again, and you just took off your Spanx and peed in the yard.

ABBIE. *Birthday Club!*

(Blackout.)

Scene Three

(Cheryl's birthday. **CHERYL, SARAH, EMILY, KATHY,** *and* **ABBIE** *are in the living room.* **KATHY** *is no longer pregnant, but she's wearing a sweater with a bulge under it that looks like she stuffed something in there. All but* **SARAH** *have wine glasses in their hands.* **SARAH** *has a glass of orange water. There's an empty coffee cup on the coffee table in front of* **KATHY.** *All but* **CHERYL** *sing the first line of "Happy Birthday.")*

ALL. *(Except* **CHERYL.***)*

HAPPY BIRTHDAY TO –

KATHY. Okay, that's good. Get 'em up.

(They raise their glasses.)

ALL. *(Except* **CHERYL.***)* To Cheryl.

ALL. Birthday Club!

(Everyone drinks except **KATHY.***)*

ALL. *(Except* **CHERYL.***)* Coasters!

(They put their glasses on coasters. **CHERYL** *is fanning herself.)*

SARAH. Before we start, can I ask a question?

CHERYL. Sure.

SARAH. Does every Birthday Club end up with somebody going to the hospital?

CHERYL. No, of course not.

EMILY. A *lot* of 'em end up that way.

CHERYL. Yeah, but not *all* of 'em.

KATHY. *(Raising her glass.)* Birthday Club: employing healthcare workers for over five years.

SARAH. You know, I just don't think Birthday Club is right for me.

KATHY. Yeah, that's what you said last time. Get over it.

SARAH. I mean, all the drinking and the peeing in the yard.

ABBIE. I just wanna say that I feel partially responsible for that.

KATHY. Did you ever get your Spanx back?

ABBIE. I think a dog run off with 'em.

SARAH. I just can't do this anymore. And Mordecai almost found out. He wanted a urine sample to see if I was on drugs.

KATHY. Oh, hey, if you ever need one, I have several in my fridge.

SARAH. I'm sorry, it's just getting out of hand.

CHERYL. I understand your apprehension, Sarah, but just pretend you're on a mission, like a Mormon mission, but instead of going to Somalia, your mission is to save our souls.

SARAH. I don't mean any disrespect, but it may be too late for that.

CHERYL. Just think about it.

EMILY. Okay, we have news. Congratulations are in order for Kathy.

KATHY. Why?

SARAH. Didn't you have a baby?

KATHY. Oh, yeah, that. Yeah, I had a girl. Or a boy. One of those.

SARAH. You don't know?

EMILY. Of course she knows. She had a girl. She's joking.

SARAH. Oh, yeah, I'm sorry, I'm just not familiar with jokes. Can you maybe raise your hand when you tell a joke, so I know?

KATHY. How about a finger?

(*Raises her middle finger.*)

SARAH. Sure, that would be fine.

KATHY. She doesn't know what that means.

ABBIE. (*To* KATHY.) How's your new baby?

KATHY. Oh, you know, like the others: eat, cry, poop, repeat.

SARAH. Where is she tonight?

KATHY. (*Points to the bump under her sweater.*) Right here.

SARAH. Your baby is under your sweater?!

KATHY. Yeah, I'm breast feeding right now.

SARAH. While you're drinking?

KATHY. Well, it's the best time. Puts her right to sleep.

SARAH. Is that good for the baby?

KATHY. Oh, yeah, wine has grapes. Although she does *not* like Merlot.

SARAH. And that's okay?

KATHY. Relax, I only drink after I'm done breastfeeding. Until then, I taste and spit.

(**KATHY** *takes a little taste of her wine, swirls it around, then spits it out in the empty coffee cup in front of her.*)

SARAH. (*Groans.*) Ohh.

KATHY. Just being responsible.

SARAH. And this is your fourth?

KATHY. That I know of.

SARAH. I want seven children.

KATHY. No, you don't.

SARAH. Are you gonna stop at four?

KATHY. I wanted to stop at zero but my husband couldn't keep his hands off his smoking hot, supermodel wife.

SARAH. Really? What's her name?

EMILY. *(After a few beats.)* Did she just make a joke?

ABBIE. I'm not sure.

SARAH. *(Realizing.)* Oh, my gosh, that was my first joke. I've never told a joke before.

(Realizing.) I'm gonna be sent to the fiery netherworld.

CHERYL. No, you won't. It was actually a pretty good joke.

KATHY. Yeah, not bad.

SARAH. As Gabrealambskafeeb said to the Mennonites, "Folly not, for merriment is an invitation to Satan's lair."

(Whispers to KATHY.) That's hell.

KATHY. We got it.

SARAH. So, where are your other children tonight?

KATHY. Two are with the babysitter and one is in juvy.

SARAH. What's "juvy"?

CHERYL. Juvenile detention center.

KATHY. It's like jail for underage kids.

SARAH. Oh, my gosh. What did he do?

KATHY. He stole a few things. Not enough to warrant going to juvy, but I made him go to teach him a lesson.

SARAH. Oh, like tough love.

KATHY. More like cruel love. He needed his butt kicked.

ABBIE. You don't think that might be a little extreme?

KATHY. Hey, that's nothing compared to what I grew up with. My dad was a tyrant. We lived in fear. But at least none of us went to jail for more than a year, so, I guess it paid off.

SARAH. Wow, I'm learning so much about you. So, where's your husband tonight?

KATHY. Oh, he's in the kitchen. Where he belongs.

SARAH. Oh, role reversal. I've heard about that.

KATHY. No, he's a chef.

SARAH. Really? Where?

KATHY. McDonald's.

SARAH. *(Not enthusiastic.)* McDonald's...great.

> *(**KATHY** raises her hand.)*

Oh, that was a joke. Okay, I'm getting it. I'm learning so much.

KATHY. Actually, he works at a really nice restaurant, Cracker Barrel.

SARAH. *(Laughs, realizes it's not a joke, then stops. To herself.)* Nope.

KATHY. *(Groans.)* Ahh! She bit my nip.

SARAH. We call that "Mother's Little Baby Nozzle."

KATHY. *(Getting up.)* Okay if I put her down?

CHERYL. Sure, use the guest bedroom.

(**KATHY** *exits down the hallway.*)

SARAH. So, Emily, how's your daughter doing?

EMILY. Oh, she's fine. She got into Stanford.

CHERYL. That's great.

EMILY. One hundred and two more days, and I'm an empty nester.

ABBIE. You know the exact number of days before she leaves?

CHERYL. I knew it down to the minute.

SARAH. Is she still gay?

EMILY. Yeah, she's…still gay.

SARAH. Well, she's young.

CHERYL. *(Changing the subject.)* So, Abbie, what's going on with you? You hanging in there?

ABBIE. Oh, you know, I'm doing the best I can, considering my husband left me.

SARAH. I'm sorry.

ABBIE. The thing is, I really like his mother. We're friends on Facebook. Can I still be friends with her?

KATHY. *(Offstage.)* Absolutely not!

ABBIE. I've been kinda depressed, so I've been going to dance therapy, trying to work through a few things.

EMILY. "Dance therapy"?

ABBIE. Thank you for asking. If it's okay, I'd like to share my feelings with you through interpretive dance.

  (**KATHY** *comes back without her "baby bump" under her sweater.*)

KATHY. Please don't.

SARAH. Sure, go ahead.

KATHY. *(Groans.)* Ahh.

ABBIE. I call this, "Melancholy."

>(**ABBIE** *proceeds to do ten seconds of the worst interpretive dance ever.)*

>*(She finishes.)*

And scene.

KATHY. My eyes just vomited.

SARAH. I think it's wonderful that you're working on yourself.

ABBIE. I bought the Tony Robbins self-help dvds.

CHERYL. Do they work?

ABBIE. I don't know. I can't seem to finish the one on procrastination.

SARAH. Well, at least you're trying.

EMILY. You need to get on Tinder.

CHERYL. Don't listen to her.

SARAH. Are you still doing that?

EMILY. I have a date this Friday, right after I get my knees botoxed.

SARAH. Whatever that is, you don't need to do that.

EMILY. It's dog eat dog out there. Should I get a Brazilian butt lift?

SARAH. What in the Jehovahmibbakabun is that?

EMILY. It's when they give you a nice little shelf back there so your man can set his beer on it.

SARAH. Why would you want a beer on your? –

CHERYL. Emily, why do you feel that you need a man?

EMILY. Oh, I don't *need* a man. I mean, I do for *some* things, but only when the batteries run out in my vibra-genie.

SARAH. And...you're getting a PhD in Education?

EMILY. Yeah, I'm looking to start a tutoring company for disadvantaged kids.

SARAH. Wow. You are a lot more impressive than most people might think.

EMILY. Thank you?

ABBIE. Hello, back to me!

CHERYL. Go ahead.

ABBIE. I met a guy.

EMILY. Really? That's great.

KATHY. Have you gone out with him?

ABBIE. Well, sort of. He's not a real, "take me to restaurants," kind of guy.

EMILY. O-kay.

ABBIE. He's a little rough around the edges, kind of earthy.

EMILY. Ooh, sounds hot.

CHERYL. Where did you meet him?

ABBIE. At the library. He was sitting on the front steps, just kind of contemplating.

SARAH. He must be smart.

KATHY. What does he do?

ABBIE. He's an outdoor consultant.

SARAH. What's that?

ABBIE. He consults outdoors.

SARAH. Still don't know what that is.

EMILY. What have you done with him?

ABBIE. I make him dinner. He's so hungry all the time.

SARAH. Ah, he loves your cooking. That's so sweet.

ABBIE. He's a great kisser.

EMILY. Well, that's important.

CHERYL. How long have you known him?

ABBIE. A few months. He likes my Spanx.

KATHY. *(Groans.)* Ohhh.

EMILY. Sounds like a keeper.

ABBIE. He's got the cutest tattoo on his forearm of a ladybug with a knife sticking through it.

EMILY. Oh, that's Jerry.

ABBIE. How do you know Jerry?

EMILY. I see him at the shelter.

ABBIE. The shelter?

EMILY. I volunteer at the homeless shelter.

SARAH. That is so sweet. I didn't know that about you.

EMILY. It's community service. I have to do it.

SARAH. Why?

EMILY. You know that country song about the woman who trashes her ex's four-wheel drive because he cheated on her? Yeah, that was about me.

ABBIE. So...you work with Jerry at the shelter?

EMILY. Yeah. I feed him.

KATHY. This is awesome.

ABBIE. Okay, wait, so...

EMILY. Jerry's homeless.

CHERYL. Whoa!

SARAH. O. M. Graciousness.

CHERYL. And you've gone out how many times?

ABBIE. Five.

KATHY. This is great.

CHERYL. Where do you go?

ABBIE. Mostly my place.

EMILY. "Mostly"?

ABBIE. Always my place.

KATHY. Can I record this?

ABBIE. He told me he owns a ranch.

EMILY. He owns a packet of ranch dressing. He carries it with him for good luck.

ABBIE. *(Cries.)* Ohhh, I've seen it.

CHERYL. Is he a nice guy?

ABBIE. Yeah.

SARAH. That's important.

KATHY. Have you done anything with him, you know, like...

    ('70s porn music-esque.) Brown chicken brown cow.

ABBIE. *(Emotional.)* We've done a lot of things... Last week he ate lasagna off of me.

EMILY. You mean off your...

    (EMILY *motions to her stomach/chest area.)*

ABBIE. *(Cries.)* Yes.

EMILY. Wow. Even *I* haven't done that.

ABBIE. *(Cries.)* Ohhh.

SARAH. Abbie, don't beat yourself up. As Nefreetieganesh said to Gabashtrazebb, "Nourish thine who are needy, for food tastes better when shared off your abdomen."

> *(Thinks.)*

That doesn't sound right.

KATHY. Moving on.

ABBIE. Wait a minute, it can't be the same Jerry that you know. This Jerry has a cell phone. Homeless guys don't have cell phones.

KATHY. Yeah, they do.

EMILY. Have you seen his cell phone?

ABBIE. No, but he gave me his number.

KATHY. What is it?

> **(ABBIE** *shows it to her on her cell phone.)*

Let me see that.

> **(KATHY** *takes* **ABBIE***'s phone and calls the number.)*

ABBIE. What are you doing?

KATHY. Hi, is this Jerry?... No? Who is this?... "Pork Chop." Your name is "Pork Chop"?... I must have the wrong number. Where am I calling?... The phone booth in front of the library? Didn't know they still had phone booths. Okay, thanks. Bye.

ABBIE. *(Crying.)* He's homeless! Oh, I am so out of practice!

> **(ABBIE** *gasps for air.)*

CHERYL. Breathe, just breathe.

ABBIE. *(Takes deep breaths, does a zen-like meditation movement with her hands.)* I am a desirable person, people love me, I will find another man, my life will go on.

(Cries.) Oh, I'm not gonna make it.

EMILY. Yes, you will.

KATHY. I'll take the under.

ABBIE. I need my husband back. I can't live without him.

CHERYL. You can't live without his stuff.

ABBIE. *(Emotional.)* I know!

SARAH. You'll be fine. As Moabickabike said to Hazeekamiffabadoo, "Those who live without, shall live within. For without they shall, but for with, they shan't.

KATHY. *(Re:* **SARAH.***)* I have no words for that.

ABBIE. I need my husband back. I can't survive without him.

CHERYL. Yes, you can.

ABBIE. Was it me? Was I not providing him with wifely services.

SARAH. As Meeshpahtoof said to the Harenganites –

KATHY. Nope.

EMILY. It wasn't you.

ABBIE. My therapist says I need to draw upon my inner strength. I'm so weak!

CHERYL. You're not weak. You're just hurt.

ABBIE. I don't know what to do.

SARAH. What would Jennifer do?

ABBIE. Jennifer?

SARAH. You started Birthday Club because of her. She must have had qualities that inspired you.

ABBIE. She did. She was really strong and independent.

EMILY. She had an amazing spirit. Nothing got her down. Not even the cancer. It was just an inconvenience to her.

KATHY. She was fearless. She would do anything on a dare.

CHERYL. She never gave up. Ever. Not even at the end.

SARAH. So, Abbie, what would Jennifer do?

ABBIE. She would suck it up.

SARAH. Then that's what you're gonna do.

(**EMILY** *sees car wash guy out the window washing his car.*)

EMILY. Car wash guy is back.

(*They all get up and look out the window.*)

CHERYL. What are the odds?

KATHY. He must know we're here.

EMILY. We need to set him up with Abbie.

SARAH. We should not be looking at him. It's wrong.

EMILY. Are you kidding? His ass is like cement.

ABBIE. His muscles have their own zip code.

EMILY. His skin is so smooth. Reminds me, I need to get a wax.

SARAH. I don't even wanna know what that is.

CHERYL. It's when they put hot wax on your –

SARAH. (*Puts fingers in her ears.*) La, la, la, la, la.

EMILY. You're close.

KATHY. *(Re: car wash guy, waving a dollar bill.)* I've got some singles, maybe we can get him to dance.

SARAH. *(To KATHY.)* Would your husband approve of you ogling car wash guy?

KATHY. He'd encourage it. Less pressure on him to perform.

SARAH. *(To CHERYL.)* Speaking of husbands, where is Dave these days?

CHERYL. Oh, he's out somewhere writing his novel.

SARAH. You haven't talked about him very much, lately.

CHERYL. Why are you badgering me about Dave?

SARAH. I'm not badgering you.

(To EMILY.) Am I badgering her?

EMILY. It's okay. It's the menopause. Hormones.

CHERYL. *(Angry.)* I am not hormonal!

SARAH. Oh, yeah, I see it now.

CHERYL. *(Angry.)* Okay, we decided to separate for awhile! Happy?!

KATHY. Again?

CHERYL. Yes.

ABBIE. Wow. Suddenly, I feel better.

CHERYL. You're welcome.

ABBIE. Oh, no, not about the separation. Okay, a little about the separation. Sorry. But, you're always so perfect. It's nice to see a flaw. Makes you human.

EMILY. What happened?

CHERYL. It's just been tough around here. He doesn't work.

SARAH. And you're a workaholic.

EMILY. He does a lot of housework. And he's working on a book.

CHERYL. The bottom line is, it's just hard to respect him.

ABBIE. Do you think the menopause had anything to do with your separation?

CHERYL. It's not the menopause!

KATHY. *(Looking at her phone.)* Sure it is. "Menopause; from the Latin word meaning, a pause from men."

CHERYL. Look, it was mutual, okay. We both needed some time apart.

ABBIE. Have you talked to him lately?

CHERYL. Not for a few days. I've been busy.

SARAH. Maybe he got in a car accident. Maybe he's in the hospital.

CHERYL. He would have called.

SARAH. Not if he was unconscious.

EMILY. He's not unconscious.

SARAH. Check your messages. See if he called.

CHERYL. Yes, Mother.

> **(CHERYL** *looks at her cell phone.)*

He sent a text.

ABBIE. Read it.

CHERYL. *(Groans.)* Ahh.

(Reads it.) "Hey, it's me. I have some good news. I finished the book. And I got a publisher."

SARAH. That's great.

CHERYL. *(Reading.)* "I'd been talking to 'em for awhile. They just wanted to see the finished book before inking the deal. And guess what, they gave me a two hundred thousand-dollar advance!"

KATHY. Holy crap.

CHERYL. *(Reading.)* "And an option on my next book."

ABBIE. Wow.

CHERYL. *(Reading.)* "Oh, and one more thing, remember when we were separated last year?... Well, while we were apart, I dated one of your friends. She's in your Birthday Club. Maybe with you right now. See ya."

(CHERYL *looks up at* **EMILY, KATHY, ABBIE,** *and* **SARAH.***)*

SARAH. Oh, crap.

(Blackout.)

ACT TWO

Scene One

(Still Cheryl's birthday, thirty seconds later. **EMILY, CHERYL, ABBIE, SARAH,** *and* **KATHY** *are in the same position as the previous scene.* **CHERYL** *is staring down her friends as they all look out, wide-eyed, avoiding eye contact with her. After an awkward pause,* **SARAH** *speaks.)*

SARAH. So...anyone have anything new they would like to share?

CHERYL. Are you serious?!

SARAH. What? We always share things that happened.

CHERYL. And right now we need to resolve something before we move on to other business.

SARAH. I'm sorry that you and your husband are separated. Shall we pray?

> *(She folds her hands,* **CHERYL** *shoots her a look.)*

Nope.

CHERYL. This is much bigger than our separation. Much, much bigger.

SARAH. What could be bigger than that?

CHERYL. Oh, sweet, sweet, Sarah. Sweet, innocent, wholesome, naive, Sarah. Never lose that.

ABBIE. It's a tough thing you're going through. I know.

CHERYL. Oh, don't patronize me. We all know what the
bigger story is. Dave dated one of you while we were
still married.

SARAH. Aren't you still married now?

CHERYL. Oh, don't get all semantics on me. We're not
together right now.

SARAH. Like last year when you were separated.

CHERYL. Okay, now you're annoying.

SARAH. Sorry, I just…but didn't you say that nothing gets
in the way of Birthday Club unless you're dead?

CHERYL. Why don't you go over there and take a little
drink of "shut your piehole"?

SARAH. Oh, is that a dessert drink?

EMILY. *(Motioning to be quiet.)* Sarah.

(**SARAH** *nods.*)

CHERYL. The bigger story is that one of you dated my
husband and we need to find out which one of you is
guilty.

ABBIE. Is that really the bigger story?

CHERYL. Rule number five: "Never brown chicken, brown
cow with another Birthday Club member's significant
other."

SARAH. Still don't know what that means.

KATHY. As Mufassa said to Dumbledore, "Never dip your
toes in your neighbor's pool."

SARAH. I don't know that one.

CHERYL. Back on topic.

SARAH. But wait, you were separated when it happened, right?

CHERYL. Okay, new girl. I think we've heard enough from you. I'd like to hear from the others.

KATHY. Pass.

CHERYL. Nope. There will be no pass.

SARAH. Well, it can't be me. I didn't even know him a year ago.

CHERYL. Okay, it's not you. So, those of you remaining, who dated my husband?

(No one answers.)

ABBIE. Well, it can't be Kathy, I mean, four kids. C'mon.

CHERYL. Yeah, you're right. He'd never go for Kathy.

KATHY. Why not? A lot of guys want me.

(SARAH laughs. KATHY shoots her a look, and she quickly stops laughing and shakes her head "no.")

CHERYL. We're not leaving until someone fesses up, so who did it?

(Slowly, EMILY raises her hand. KATHY sees her and she, too, raises her hand, then ABBIE raises her hand.)

Oh, so all three of you dated my husband? Kathy, really?

EMILY. Okay, I confess. I did it. They're covering for me.

CHERYL. Well, duh, I knew that. I mean, you're the only one he'd go for.

ABBIE. What about me?

CHERYL. You date a homeless man.

ABBIE. He likes my lasagna.

KATHY. With a pinch of breast.

CHERYL. *(To* **EMILY.***)* You are a homewrecker.

SARAH. Wasn't it wrecked before they went out?

CHERYL. *(To* **SARAH.***)* Okay, as of now, I am revoking your speaking privileges.

EMILY. I just wanna say this, we just went out one time. We didn't do anything.

CHERYL. Did you kiss him?

EMILY. *(After a beat.)* Define "kiss him."

SARAH. *(Raising her hand.)* Oh, I know this one. When your lips touch in a closed manner for under five seconds.

EMILY. Nope. We did not do that.

CHERYL. You kissed him!

EMILY. Not according to the Heemish.

CHERYL. That's not how people kiss.

SARAH. It isn't?

EMILY. At the time, he said it was over, that you kicked him out. Wasn't that true?

CHERYL. Don't you dare use logic on me.

EMILY. I'm sorry. I felt horrible when you got back together. Not because you were back together, but because we kissed.

CHERYL. So you did kiss!

SARAH. In the book of Habinnaminnafiff it says that forgiveness is the pathway to joyful cornhusking.

CHERYL. Nobody asked you.

SARAH. But you said I'm on a mission to save your soul.

ABBIE. You did say that.

CHERYL. Dammit.

SARAH. Language. And one thing you taught me is nothing can break up Birthday Club. We will get through this. As Miffaposhminock said to Gafeetiesiffmabet, "Discontent forges the broken limb."

KATHY. Would you just knock it off with – wait, that one actually made sense.

CHERYL. I'm sorry, but Birthday Club is over.

ABBIE. Why?

CHERYL. Conflict between members. Falls under "special provisions." It's in the addendum.

SARAH. Would Jennifer want you to quit?

CHERYL. Don't bring in Jennifer.

ABBIE. No, she would not want us to quit.

SARAH. Okay, then. I make a motion to add a new rule.

EMILY. Second.

SARAH. Rule number nine: "No conflict shall disrupt Birthday Club. All conflicts between members must be resolved." All those in favor?

ALLL. *(Except **CHERYL.** All but **CHERYL** raise their hands.)* Aye.

SARAH. A majority. Rule number nine is ratified, Birthday Club will continue, and you will resolve your conflict.

CHERYL. *(Giving in.)* Recognized. Under protest.

SARAH. Thanks.

CHERYL. *(To **EMILY**.)* But this is not over. The rule says, we "will resolve" our conflict. It's not resolved yet.

EMILY. Got it.

ABBIE. Good. Now, on to business. Emily?

EMILY. Well, I stopped going to yoga, and started going to liposuction. It's much easier.

ABBIE. Didn't you have a new Tinder date the other night?

EMILY. Yeah, Maserati. We had three bottles of wine. It was crazy.

KATHY. My husband and I have a strict limit, two bottles of wine a night. And then we go to vodka.

SARAH. That's a lot of alcohol.

(**KATHY** *raises her hand.*)

Oh, a joke. Hey, I got one. How do you please an Amish woman?

KATHY. No idea.

SARAH. Two Mennonite.

(*They look straight-faced at* **SARAH** *for a few beats.*)

Get it? Two men a night...

(*All still straight-faced.*)

'Cause a Mennonite is a, you know –

KATHY. Yeah, we got it.

EMILY. It was a nice effort.

ABBIE. I thought it was funny.

KATHY. Keep trying.

(*Her phone vibrates.*)

Excuse me.

(On the phone.) Listen honey, Mommy needs some alone time right now.

(Takes a little drink.)

No, I can't be interrupted. What I'm doing is very important.

(Takes another drink.)

I'll call you when I'm done. In the meantime, lose my phone number.

(She hangs up.)

SARAH. You know, you attract more bees with honey than with vinegar.

KATHY. How would you like some vinegar in your "exit only"?

SARAH. You know, we all love you, right?

ABBIE. We do.

KATHY. Stop it.

SARAH. And your kids love you, too. And they need you to be there for them.

KATHY. They're fine on their own.

CHERYL. *(To* SARAH, *re:* KATHY.*)* Is this part of your soul saving mission?

SARAH. It is. It's kind of fun.

(To KATHY.*)* You should do something nice for your kids. Take 'em on a vacation. They would love that.

KATHY. Are you insane?

SARAH. I think someone needs a hug.

(SARAH goes to hug KATHY.)

KATHY. Don't even think about it.

    (SARAH stops.)

ABBIE. I'll take a hug.

SARAH. *(To* **KATHY.***)* Well, then hug your kids. They need your love and support. Just like Emily's daughter in her time of discovery.

EMILY. Say what now?

SARAH. She's young. She's still learning about herself and making life choices. She's confused.

EMILY. About being gay? That's not a choice. I mean, she's confused, but not about that.

CHERYL. She was born that way.

SARAH. Huh. That's not what they taught us in suppression education.

KATHY. I'm guessing there's a lot they didn't teach you.

EMILY. And we're gonna help you with that.

SARAH. What do you mean?

EMILY. Your wedding is coming up pretty soon, right?

SARAH. In two months.

EMILY. And you want to be prepared for your wedding night, don't you?

SARAH. Well, sure, it's my duty as a wife subordinate.

KATHY. So sad.

EMILY. Well, this is your lucky day, because today we are throwing you a bachelorette party, and you're gonna learn everything you need to know for that special night.

SARAH. Oh, I don't know about this.

EMILY. Okay, we're gonna start with some games. We've got Pin the Pistol on the Cowboy, Toilet Paper Lingerie, and a special treat later. We're also gonna show you the proper way of kissing. But first, a game called "Finish the Sentence." Are you ready?

ABBIE. I'm ready.

SARAH. Before we start, can I spend five minutes in the repent corner?

EMILY. No. Okay, here we go.

(*Looking at her cell phone.*) On my wedding night, I'm looking forward to losing my...

SARAH. Hand sanitizer.

CHERYL. "Hand sanitizer"?

SARAH. We make it out of lye soap and prayers.

KATHY. Did you understand the question?

SARAH. Yes, I'm just gonna throw caution to the wind on my wedding night, and after my initial scrub down, I will not cleanse again until after the post-coitus shame prayers.

KATHY. Strangely, this is going exactly how I thought it would.

EMILY. (*Reading.*) Next question: On my wedding night, I will be wearing nothing but...

SARAH. A flannel isolation gown. Stitched on a handloom by farm spinsters.

CHERYL. Don't you wanna wear something sexy for your new husband?

SARAH. Oh, he'll be in the other room.

KATHY. Maybe we should go to the next game.

EMILY. (*Reading.*) Couple more. If you stand outside my bedroom on my wedding night, you'll hear...

SARAH. *The Golden Girls.* Your wedding night is the one
    time you're allowed to watch TV, and I hear *The Golden
    Girls* is a great show.

ABBIE. I love *The Golden Girls.*

EMILY. I have one more –

KATHY. *(Looks at her cell phone.)* No, you don't. Time to
    move on.

    Sarah, would you like to be prepared on your wedding
    night?

SARAH. Well, yes, that's what I thought we were doing.

EMILY. We have a game that'll teach you everything you
    need to know – oh, shoot, I left it on the front porch.
    Will you get it, Sarah?

SARAH. Sure.

    (She goes to the door.)

    I love games. Especially *(Does the hand gesture.)* "Rock,
    Paper, Sheep shears."

    (She opens the front door and looks out.)

    I don't see it – oh, my gosh, there's a man out here. All
    he's wearing are cowboy boots and a holster, holding a
    cowboy hat over his – all my senses are exploding!

KATHY. His name is Dusty.

SARAH. Hi, Dusty.

    (Looks down at his hat.) Oh, he's removing his hat! Oh,
    my eyes! My eyes are burning! What is that between
    his – Is that real?! That can *not* be real! That is *not*
    what it looks like in the anatomy book stick figures!

    (Puts hand over her eyes.) Oh, they're gonna send me
    to the dirty-thought spank room!

EMILY. I wanna go there!

CHERYL, EMILY, ABBIE & KATHY. *Birthday Club!*

(Blackout.)

Scene Two

(Sarah's birthday. **CHERYL, EMILY, ABBIE, KATHY,** *and* **SARAH** *are seated with wine glasses in their hands.* **SARAH** *has orange water.* **CHERYL** *is fanning herself while* **SARAH** *sings the last line of "Happy Birthday" as she cries.)*

SARAH. *(Singing, while crying.)*
HAPPY BIRTHDAY TO ME.

ALL. *(Except* **SARAH.** *Unenthusiastic.)* Birthday Club.

*(***CHERYL, EMILY, ABBIE,** *and* **KATHY** *take a drink.)*

CHERYL. Okay. Anyone wanna share anything?

*(***SARAH** *raises her hand,* **CHERYL** *ignores her.)*

Anyone at all?

*(***SARAH** *waves her hand,* **CHERYL** *ignores her.)*

Anyone?

*(***SARAH** *waves her hand harder.* **CHERYL** *finally gives in.)*

Sarah.

SARAH. *(Crying.)* It's over with Mordecai.

KATHY. Who would have guessed?

ABBIE. I did. I guessed it.

EMILY. What happened?

SARAH. Well, after the bachelorette party, I saw him and I…

(To herself.) I am so ashamed.

(To the others.) I tried to kiss him like they do in France.

EMILY. He didn't like it?

SARAH. He threw up.

ABBIE. I've had worse.

SARAH. Then he said I was morally corrupt and he called me a harpy, and then he went to the church silo to thrash his knuckles.

KATHY. You sure that was the only thing he was thrashing?

CHERYL. So, what are you gonna do?

SARAH. He says if I don't quit Birthday Club today, it's over between us.

EMILY. The ultimatum.

SARAH. He's right, I'm not the same person I was when I joined. I'm a degenerate now. I got a Sears catalogue so I could look at the men's underwear ads.

ABBIE. I used to do that.

SARAH. The elders banished me from the Saturday night knitting circle and made me apologize to the entire flock.

ABBIE. To the congregation?

SARAH. No, a flock of sheep. It's symbolic.

KATHY. I don't think she's joking.

SARAH. I'm a shame to the Heemish. I'm shame-ish.

CHERYL. Any advice for Sarah?

KATHY. I've got nothin'.

(*Looks at* **EMILY** *and* **ABBIE**.) Anyone?

(**ABBIE** *shakes her head.*)

EMILY. We're rooting for you?

CHERYL. (*To* **SARAH**.) Okay, we're gonna put a pin in that, and we'll get back to you.

CHERYL. *(Changing the subject.)* Any other news?

ABBIE. I'm seeing someone.

KATHY. This should be good.

EMILY. Who is he? What does he do?

ABBIE. He's an aquatic engineer.

SARAH. Ooh, sounds fancy.

EMILY. Where did you meet him?

ABBIE. In my back yard.

EMILY. What was he doing there?

ABBIE. Working on the pool.

CHERYL. He's your pool boy?

ABBIE. Well, he's twenty-four, so I guess technically, he's a boy.

KATHY. Oh, dear Lord.

SARAH. And you're seeing him?

ABBIE. Yeah, I see him in the backyard.

KATHY. Do you hear yourself?

CHERYL. I don't think that really counts as "seeing him."

ABBIE. The other day, he looked at me wantingly.

EMILY. How do you know it was, "wantingly"?

ABBIE. I just know. I've gotten that look from other men.

KATHY. Show us the look.

>(**ABBIE** *shows them a strained, awkward look.*)

Was he constipated?

ABBIE. No.

CHERYL. What happened next?

ABBIE. He asked to use the bathroom...oh, yeah, why didn't I see that?

EMILY. You have to admire her blind optimism.

ABBIE. He's so cute. What should I do?

KATHY. Give him some Ex-Lax?

ABBIE. *(Cries.)* Ohhh. I've been trying so hard to put up a brave front, and hide my inner feelings.

KATHY. *(Re: her crying.)* Have you?

ABBIE. It's just that...I'm losing the house.

SARAH. You're what? How did that happen?

ABBIE. It's in the prenup.

EMILY. You signed a prenup?

ABBIE. I love my house.

SARAH. It has four pocket doors.

CHERYL. What are you gonna do?

ABBIE. I'm gonna make one last attempt to get him back. I'm goin' for the Hail Mary.

KATHY. What if it doesn't work?

ABBIE. I don't know, I guess I'll move back to Nebraska to live with my mom.

EMILY. You're not gonna fight it?

ABBIE. It's in the prenup.

EMILY. So? Prenups get broken all the time. Listen, I've got a great attorney. I'll text you his contact info. Tell him "Sadusa" referred you.

ABBIE. "Sadusa"?

EMILY. He'll know.

ABBIE. You know what, I'm gonna call my husband. I'm gonna throw that Hail Mary right now. I mean, why wait, right?

(ABBIE *hits speed dial on her phone.*)

KATHY. This is not gonna end well.

ABBIE. *(Into phone.)* Hey, it's me. How you doin'?... Yeah, I'm good. Hey listen, I was thinking about you the other day. I got these tickets to, ahhh...

(She thinks.)

To the World Series, game four... I know, how did I get 'em, right?

(Covers the phone, whispers to the others.) I don't really have them.

KATHY. *(Whispers back.)* We know.

ABBIE. *(Back to her husband.)* Yeah, two tickets, and I was wondering if you'd like to go... You would? Really?... Awesome!... Sure...yeah...okay, good talking to you. Bye.

(ABBIE *hangs up.*)

EMILY. Well, that sounded promising.

ABBIE. He wants me to drop the tickets off so he can take his girlfriend.

KATHY. I had my money on that.

SARAH. That's not what you wanted, right?

ABBIE. *(Cries.)* NO!

CHERYL. What are you gonna do?

ABBIE. Leave the country.

KATHY. Okay, not a Cinderella moment. Anyone have anything positive to share?

SARAH. So, Emily, I hear you're dating someone new.

EMILY. Beemer.

ABBIE. How's that going?

EMILY. I broke up with him.

CHERYL. What happened? I thought this was the one. You've been going out for, like, three months.

KATHY. Which in Emily time is ten years.

EMILY. What happened? What always happens? He was fun and cute and everything, but every time we went out, my brain cells would deteriorate.

CHERYL. Not a genius?

EMILY. He has to get naked to be able to count to twenty-one.

SARAH. *(Thinks.)* I don't get it.

KATHY. Any other good news?

CHERYL. Dave served me the divorce papers.

KATHY. Oh, that's uplifting.

EMILY. Do you need a good attorney?

CHERYL. No, I'm not gonna fight it.

EMILY. You should get half of his two hundred thousand advance.

CHERYL. I don't want it.

EMILY. Are you kidding? You inspired him to write his novel. I mean, if you weren't such an anal-retentive, rules-oriented, clean slash control freak, he wouldn't have written the book.

CHERYL. I know there's a compliment in there somewhere, but I only have myself to blame.

KATHY. Never blame yourself! Ever! Especially if it's your fault.

SARAH. That doesn't sound healthy.

EMILY. What about the house?

CHERYL. I bought it. He's not contesting it.

EMILY. Okay, good. At least you won't be homeless.

ABBIE. *(Cries.)* Ohhh!

EMILY. Does anyone have any good news?

KATHY. My son is out of juvy.

CHERYL. Great.

KATHY. Yeah, he wants to move in with his grandparents.

ABBIE. That's not good. Is it?

KATHY. You know what I realized. I am not a good mother.

(Nobody says anything.)

Nobody is gonna argue with me?

EMILY. Well...

SARAH. You know, I bet you have some good qualities as a mother.

KATHY. Last Tuesday, I left my daughter at the grocery store. For the third time. Good thing I knew the cop that brought her home.

SARAH. See? Happy ending.

KATHY. My baby girl's first word was "cabernet."

SARAH. It's a hard word. She must be smart.

KATHY. Or, I shouldn't drink wine while holding my baby.

SARAH. Easy mistake.

KATHY. Child services has me on speed dial.

SARAH. To let you know what a wonderful mother you are.

KATHY. You know, I appreciate it, Sarah, but you can't make a silk purse out of a sow's ear.

SARAH. Oh, yes, you can. We do it every Sunday in the town square after the pig races.

KATHY. Nothing you say surprises me anymore.

SARAH. Where's your husband in all this?

KATHY. He works every night. He's never home when they're home.

SARAH. Do you have pictures of your kids?

(**KATHY** *hands her cell phone to* **SARAH.** **SARAH** *looks at the pictures.*)

Oh, how cute.

(**SARAH** *types a text on* **KATHY**'s *phone.*)

KATHY. What are you doing?

SARAH. Nothing.

KATHY. You're typing something.

SARAH. I'm just looking at the pictures.

KATHY. While typing. Stop that.

SARAH. And send.

(**SARAH** *hits* "send.")

KATHY. What did you do?

(**KATHY** *grabs the phone back and reads the text* **SARAH** *sent.*)

(*Reading.*) You sent them a text?

ABBIE. (*To* **SARAH.**) How do you know how to use a cell phone?

SARAH. Cheryl taught me at work.

EMILY. *(To* **KATHY.***)* What did she say?

KATHY. *(Reading.)* "Hey, kids. So sorry Dad and I haven't spent more time with you. We love you so much and we'd like to make it up to you by taking you some place special."

(To **SARAH.***)* They'll never believe this is from me.

SARAH. They'll wanna believe it. Take 'em to Disney World. They'll love you for it.

KATHY. No way.

ABBIE. It's the happiest place on earth.

KATHY. I hate happiness.

SARAH. I always wanted to go to Disney World when I was growing up, but they wouldn't let us.

CHERYL. You're really stirring the pot tonight.

SARAH. I guess I just wanted to go out with a bang. That's a saying, right?

CHERYL. You're, what now?

SARAH. I'm sorry, but this is my last Birthday Club.

EMILY. You say that every time.

SARAH. This time I'm serious. I thought I worked things out with Mordecai, but he told the elders about Birthday Club. And if I don't quit today, they'll banish me from the flock.

KATHY. Of sheep?

SARAH. No, that would be weird.

EMILY. So, is this final?

SARAH. I'm afraid so.

(To **CHERYL.***)* I'm sorry. I hope this won't hurt my working for you.

CHERYL. No. In fact I wanna promote you. Put you in charge of the West Coast.

SARAH. Really? Wow. What does that entail?

CHERYL. Well, more responsibility, and you'll have five people reporting to you.

SARAH. Will any of them be men?

CHERYL. Yeah, ahh, three. Three men.

SARAH. Oooh. Yeah, they don't allow us to have men reporting to women.

CHERYL. Are you serious?

EMILY. That's ridiculous.

KATHY. C'mon, even Jesus reported to a woman, and apparently she worked him pretty hard.

ABBIE. That doesn't sound right.

KATHY. Oh, yeah, it's in the Bible. It says that Mary rode Jesus' ass all the way to Bethlehem.

ABBIE. That was Joseph. And she rode his donkey.

KATHY. Oh. That explains a lot.

SARAH. I'm sorry, but I have to decline the offer. Thank you, though.

CHERYL. They really ask you to sacrifice a lot, don't they.

SARAH. Yeah, they do. I mean, you know what it's like to make sacrifices for work.

CHERYL. Yeah, I guess I kinda worked myself out of my marriage.

EMILY. Do you miss him?

CHERYL. Yeah, I do.

ABBIE. Call him, tell him you haven't been yourself. Blame it on the menopause.

CHERYL. No, I'm not gonna do that.

EMILY. You wanna continue to be his friend, don't you? I mean, you have two daughters together. Call him.

CHERYL. *(Speed dialing her phone.)* You guys are relentless.

(On the phone.) Went to voicemail… Hey, it's me. Look, I'm really proud that you got your book published. And I'm sorry I've been kind of a jerk this last year. It's the menopause… Yeah, no, it isn't. It's just me. Look, you're a good person. I'll sign the divorce papers. You deserve better. Take care.

> *(**CHERYL** hangs up.)*

KATHY. Well, tonight has been one gigantic crap fest.

CHERYL. You know, maybe it's time we end Birthday Club.

KATHY. No, we can't do that. I look forward to being away from my kids. Don't take that away from me.

CHERYL. Birthday Club is about helping each other get through tough times, and that's not happening right now. It's not working.

SARAH. Would Jennifer want you to end Birthday Club?

CHERYL. Jennifer is better than me.

SARAH. Don't say that.

CHERYL. I was with Jennifer the day before she died. I never told anyone this, but she asked me how I was doing. I started telling her about work and all the problems I had to deal with. And as sick as she was, she actually listened, and even helped me with something I was struggling with. Helping *me* out, while *she* was dying.

(Emotional.) And the whole time I was there, I never asked her how *she* was doing. Whether *she* needed anything. It was all about *me*... How can anyone be so selfish?

EMILY. Just you being there meant so much to her. You know that.

CHERYL. I'm sorry, I just... I don't like myself very much right now.

EMILY. Cheryl –

CHERYL. Look, I appreciate it, but... I just need to take some time off to rethink my priorities.

ABBIE. *(Standing up.)* We are not giving up! We're not gonna lose this battle! We're gonna fight this! We're gonna take it to the streets! Who's with me?!

> (**ABBIE** *runs outside. Nobody goes with her. She comes back in.*)

Who's with me?

KATHY. You need to work on "reading the room."

ABBIE. Okay, plan B. I'm calling Jerry.

> (**ABBIE** *takes out her cell phone and punches in a number.*)

SARAH. The homeless guy?

ABBIE. If this is our last Birthday Club, I'm going out with a bang, too.

(Into the phone.) Hello, Jerry?... Oh, hey, you're home.

KATHY. Say hi to Pork Chop.

ABBIE. *(Into phone.)* It's Abbie. Hey, are you hungry?... Why don't I pick you up. Make you dinner.

KATHY. Don't do it, Abbie.

ABBIE. *(Into phone.)* Sounds good. See you in a half hour.

KATHY. He used you as a dinner plate.

EMILY. At least he'll wash the dishes.

ABBIE. *(Into phone.)* Oh, hey, I'm wearing my Spanx.

KATHY. Someone please stop her.

ABBIE. I'll send you a photo of what to expect.

> (**ABBIE** *sticks her butt out and takes a photo of it.)*

EMILY. Hard to stop a runaway train.

> (**ABBIE** *sends the photo to Jerry.)*

ABBIE. And send.

KATHY. You just texted your butt to a *pay phone.*

ABBIE. *Birthday Club!*

> *(Blackout.)*

Scene Three

*(Emily's birthday. **CHERYL** is sitting on the couch by herself, holding a glass of wine. Three empty wine glasses sit on the bar next to a bottle of wine. Nobody else is in the room. She finishes singing the last line of "Happy Birthday.")*

CHERYL. *(Singing, unenthusiastically.)*
HAPPY BIRTHDAY TO YOU.

(Raises her glass, unenthusiastic.) Birthday Club.

(To herself.) Anyone like to share anything that happened since last time?... Cheryl?... Who, me? Oh, okay... Well, I'm a total mess, I lost my husband, I screwed up Birthday Club, I don't have any friends anymore...

*(**EMILY** enters.)*

EMILY. Knock, knock.

CHERYL. What are you doing here?

EMILY. It's my birthday. Isn't this Birthday Club?

CHERYL. I thought we were taking a break.

EMILY. Well, we didn't vote on it, so it would be against the law to break up Birthday Club until we do.

CHERYL. Right, good point. We wouldn't wanna break the law.

*(**KATHY** and **ABBIE** enter.)*

ABBIE. Is this the right place?

CHERYL. So much for anyone listening to me.

KATHY. Why would we start now?

(They both go to the bar and pour themselves a glass of wine.)

EMILY. Well, it looks like a quorum. I guess we can officially conduct business.

KATHY. I make a motion that we start drinking.

EMILY. Second.

ABBIE. Where's Sarah?

CHERYL. I don't think she'll be here.

(From outside, they hear the first line of:)

SARAH. *(Offstage.)*

OH, WHEN THE SAINTS GO MARCHING IN.

(She enters the house.)

OH, WHEN THE SAINTS GO MARCHING IN.

KATHY. I thought singing joyously was a sin.

SARAH. It is.

*(**ABBIE** walks behind the couch and spills some of her wine.)*

ABBIE. Oh, my gosh, I spilled.

CHERYL. You what?!

*(**CHERYL** jumps up to look.)*

SARAH. Clean it up, fast.

EMILY. I'll get a towel.

KATHY. I'll get the disinfectant.

CHERYL. Stop!

*(They all stop. **CHERYL** stares at the spill.)*

ABBIE. Please don't hurt me. I'll clean it up. I promise.

CHERYL. Do not touch the spill!

EMILY. What's happening?

KATHY. I think she's having a stroke.

ABBIE. I'm scared.

SARAH. Someone do something.

CHERYL. No!

SARAH. Should I call 9-1-1?

EMILY. Yes.

CHERYL. Do not call 9-1-1.

SARAH. I don't feel safe.

ABBIE. What should we do with the spill?

CHERYL. Step. Away. From the spill.

KATHY. She's in shock.

ABBIE. Are you sick? Do you need a doctor?

CHERYL. I'm not sick. I just don't wanna clean the spill.

EMILY. *(Soothing her.)* Okay, okay, everything is gonna be alright. We'll move away from the spill.

CHERYL. Let's all just relax.

ABBIE. Sure, sure. We'll relax.

(They all sit.)

SARAH. Are we still using coasters?

CHERYL. Well, yeah. We're not barbarians.

ABBIE. She sounds better. Good.

CHERYL. Let's just move on to business.

KATHY. One second, I'm gettin' a call.

(Looks at her cell phone.) Oh, it's my daughter. I should probably take this.

CHERYL. How are your kids?

KATHY. Why? What did you hear?

CHERYL. Nothing. I'm just asking.

KATHY. They're fine. I think. I'll let you know.

(*Answers phone.*) Hi, honey, what's up?... Yes, I'll bring you some Fruit Loops... Yeah, we can go to the park tomorrow. Anything else?... Okay, I love you. Bye, bye.

ABBIE. Did you just use the "L" word with your daughter. Out loud?

EMILY. Are we in "opposite world"?

KATHY. Yeah, those little extortionists finally got to me.

SARAH. How? What happened?

KATHY. I was losing 'em. I needed to reconnect. So, my husband and I took 'em to Disney World.

CHERYL. Wow, that's huge.

SARAH. The happiest –

KATHY. Don't say it. All those disgustingly happy people with their families having fun.

(*To* SARAH.) And it's all your fault.

SARAH. It is?

KATHY. I have one thing to say to you.

SARAH. Uh-oh.

KATHY. (*A beat.*) Thanks.

SARAH. For what?

KATHY. For being such a dork.

SARAH. You're...welcome?

KATHY. They had a great time. They loved it.

SARAH. What made you change your mind?

KATHY. Well, one day my second youngest came up to me and she said, "Mommy, you're always so sad all the time...Is it my fault?... Did I do something to make you sad?

(*Emotional.*) 'Cause if I did, I'm sorry. I promise I'll be better. I promise I'll never do it again. I just want you to be happy, Mommy." And then she said, "Just know that, no matter what, I love you."

SARAH. Wow.

ABBIE. (*Emotional.*) I think I'm gonna cry.

KATHY. That was a game changer.

CHERYL. No kidding.

KATHY. I don't know. I guess I loved 'em or something. I know, it's a sign of weakness.

SARAH. No, it isn't.

KATHY. If you tell anyone I said that, you'll never see your cat again.

SARAH. How do you know I have a cat?

KATHY. His name is Jedamathiafab. He likes yarn balls and chasing squirrels...

(*She puts her index and middle fingers to her eyes, then points to* **SARAH**, *"I'm watching you."*)

And by the way, that's how I was raised, okay. My parents never showed affection or took us anywhere.

ABBIE. And you overcame it. Good for you.

EMILY. We're proud of you.

KATHY. Bite me.

CHERYL. And she's back.

KATHY. I don't know why you guys put up with me. Sometimes I just don't feel like I fit in here.

SARAH. What about *me*? *I'm* the outlier.

ABBIE. I thought *I* was.

SARAH. The thing is, we're all different, and we all have flaws. And I think that's why we keep coming back. Not just for support, but to learn and grow from our differences and become better people. And it's working. I mean, Kathy is almost human now.

KATHY. *(Gushes, to* **SARAH.***)* Ohh… I love hate you.

EMILY. That was nice, Sarah… So, how's Mordecai?

SARAH. We broke up.

CHERYL. What?!

SARAH. Oh, I don't know, Mordecai is a good person. And we'll always be friends, but we're just different. I mean, I'll always love him, but in a Heemish, like a cousin, kind of love.

EMILY. Don't the Heemish marry their cousins?

SARAH. Right. Okay, that's not a good example.

ABBIE. Breaking up with Mordecai. That is huge.

SARAH. Well, it turns out that he was gay. So there's that, too.

EMILY. That explains a few things.

SARAH. He said he was born that way. I guess the Heemish got it wrong.

KATHY. You think?

SARAH. Seems like they get a lot of things wrong. So, I left the Heemish religion.

ABBIE. Really?!

SARAH. Oh, it was mutual. They just have so many rules. No TV, no cell phones, no zippers. The worst is no drinking. I love to drink, thanks to you guys. Dammit.

ABBIE. Did you just swear?

SARAH. Yes. It feels so...rebelious.

CHERYL. So, what now?

SARAH. I'm a Lutheran now. They don't have as many rules. I mean, you still can't kill people. And they have these other commandments. But I can watch *The Golden Girls* all I want.

ABBIE. *Golden Girls*!

SARAH. So, Cheryl, if that promotion is still available, I can have men report to me now.

CHERYL. You got it. It's yours.

SARAH. Thank you... Okay, enough about me. So, Abbie, how did things go with Jerry?

ABBIE. Oh, yeah, I ended up taking him to Cracker Barrel, then drove him home. I see him every week.

KATHY. Well, if that's what you want, we're with you.

ABBIE. Oh, we're just friends. I started to volunteer at the shelter.

EMILY. Good for you.

ABBIE. *(Takes out her cell phone.)* Oh, I'm gettin' a call.

(Looks at phone.) It's my husband.

KATHY. Put it on speaker.

ABBIE. No.

(Into phone.) Hey, what's up?... Yeah, I'm sorry, too. I wish things had turned out differently... You what?... You wanna get back together? Give it another shot?

(Does a fist pump and mouths "Yes!")

ABBIE. Wow. That is...that's really unexpected. What about the nurse?... Uh-huh...well that's too bad. I mean, she was so young and hot, and that you would want me back is great... No, I mean it... So, here's the deal, I don't wanna get back together with you... Because you're a jerk. You cheated on me and you suck, and you don't deserve me. I'm a much better person without you. I have an identity, self esteem, I love myself. And I owe it all to my friends, and not to you, you big buttface. But thank you, though, for the opportunity to grace myself with your presence. Buh bye.

*(**ABBIE** hangs up.)*

(They all slow clap and give her a standing ovation.)

KATHY. You are my new hero.

EMILY. Your face should be on Mount Rushmore. Right next to Oprah's.

CHERYL. I just think it's really brave that you walked away from such a nice lifestyle.

ABBIE. Oh, I didn't walk away from anything. I called Emily's attorney. I got the house. And half of everything.

EMILY. That's awesome. I'm glad it worked out.

ABBIE. Are you dating him?

EMILY. Oh, no, we're just friends.

ABBIE. So, would it be okay if I went out with him?

EMILY. Absolutely.

ABBIE. Great, thanks. Because we've already gone out, like, three times. And he was amazing.

('70s porn music-esque.) Brown chicken, brown cow.

EMILY. Good for you.

ABBIE. What can I say? I love pocket doors more than my husband.

CHERYL. You are an inspiration.

KATHY. A Joan of Arc.

SARAH. A modern day Hebidifemmah, daughter of Mafibasheff.

KATHY. Speaking of which, any more Tinder dates, Emily?

EMILY. No, I'm taking a break from dating.

KATHY. What?! Are you dying?

EMILY. No. I started my company, City Prep Tutoring, and it's beginning to take off.

ABBIE. So, no more dating?

EMILY. I just don't have the time. Besides, I just got tired of the whole dating scene. It just felt so empty. Plus I'm getting older. I used to go out at ten. Now I go to bed at ten.

CHERYL. The other night I fixed myself a Metamucil and vodka.

KATHY. I usually go with gin.

CHERYL. *(To* **EMILY.***)* Are you happy?

EMILY. Yeah, I'm really happy. It sounds corny, but I love helping these students, you know, to have a better chance in life. I feel like I'm making a difference.

KATHY. You're right, that sounds corny.

EMILY. Plus, I don't have to look nice all the time, I save money on botox, and I can eat ice cream.

SARAH. I make ice cream. Lemon potato. I'll bring some.

KATHY. We'll make vodka floats.

EMILY. So, Cheryl, what's going on with Dave?

CHERYL. Well, I sent him the divorce papers.

EMILY. Are you okay with that?

CHERYL. Not really. But it was out of my control.

ABBIE. That's a first.

CHERYL. Okay, I get it. I'm a little controlling. A lot controlling. But I have responsibilities: a company to run, a mortgage, two girls in college. And this frigging menopause is making me crazy.

(*Realizing.*) Oh, my gosh, what if the menopause doesn't exist and this is the real me?

KATHY. You're just *now* figuring that out?

EMILY. You know what, you're gonna be alright. We're gonna help you get through this.

CHERYL. Thanks.

EMILY. Would you go back to him?

ABBIE. He's working, making money.

CHERYL. It's not my decision. The bottom line is, he left.

EMILY. The bottom line is, think with your heart, not with your head.

CHERYL. You get that on the bottom of a Snapple cap?

EMILY. Look, I'm sorry I went out with your husband three times.

CHERYL. I thought it was once.

EMILY. (*Thinks.*) The point is, it doesn't matter. We didn't do anything.

CHERYL. You kissed.

EMILY. (*Thinks.*) The point is, he loves you. He just sometimes felt emasculated around you.

CHERYL. Yeah, I guess I need to work on that.

EMILY. Do you love him?

CHERYL. Yeah, I do. You were right, he's been really supportive, and loving, and a great father, and he cleans the gutters.

EMILY. *(Into phone.)* Did you hear that?... The whole thing?

(To **CHERYL.***)* He heard you.

CHERYL. Dave was listening?

EMILY. Yeah.

CHERYL. Is that even legal?

EMILY. Probably not. Look, he wants to come back.

CHERYL. Why?

EMILY. Because he loves you and you inspire him. You and your anal-retentive, clean slash control freak –

CHERYL. Okay, okay.

EMILY. So, do you want him back?

CHERYL. Yes.

EMILY. Then tell him. In person. He's ten minutes away.

CHERYL. I'm gonna kill you.

EMILY. It's Birthday Club.

(Into phone.) Come on over... Okay, see you soon.

*(***EMILY*** hangs up.)*

KATHY. Well, this should be fun.

CHERYL. *(To* **EMILY.***)* You suck. I mean, you're a good friend and everything, but you really suck.

EMILY. You're welcome.

ABBIE. Okay, any other good news?

(*SARAH looks out the window.*)

SARAH. I met someone.

ABBIE. Really? Who?

(*EMILY looks out the window and sees car wash guy.*)

EMILY. Car wash guy is back.

SARAH. His name is Jason.

(*They look out the window and see car wash guy. SARAH waves.*)

EMILY. He totally knows we're here.

KATHY. He's looking.

(*They all duck except SARAH.*)

CHERYL. What are you doing? Get down. He'll see you.

SARAH. That's okay. He *has* seen me.

EMILY. Wait. You're going out with car wash guy?

SARAH. Jason.

KATHY. Holy crap.

SARAH. We kiss like they do in France.

(*They all stand back up and look out.*)

ABBIE. No way.

SARAH. And we did that whole brown cow chicken dance.

CHERYL. Are you serious?!

EMILY. Oh, you have *got* to give us the details!

(*SARAH raises her hand.*)

KATHY. She was joking. Holy crap.

SARAH. *(Laughs.)* We never went out.

CHERYL. Wow. That was impressive.

KATHY. We've created a monster.

SARAH. I'm gonna flash him.

KATHY. Hell, yeah!

CHERYL. Do you even know what that means?

SARAH. Yes, it means exposing yourself.

CHERYL. That is not a good idea.

EMILY. Yes, it is.

KATHY. Do it!

CHERYL. Please don't.

KATHY. I dare you.

ABBIE. What would Jennifer do?

KATHY. She'd go the Full Monty!

EMILY. What are you waiting for?

SARAH. I've never done this before.

CHERYL. This is not gonna end well.

SARAH. Ready for the Full Montague?! *(Pronounced "Mon-ta-gyou.")*

KATHY. Can't even get *that* right.

SARAH. Feast your eyes, car wash guy!

> *(She lifts up her shirt. Underneath is what looks like a giant orthopedic body brace. The Heemish version of a bra.)*

(Yelling.) Ahhhhhhhhhhhhhh!

EMILY. *(Re:* **SARAH***'s "bra.")* What are you wearing?

KATHY. It looks like a giant orthopedic body brace.

SARAH. It's my bra.

EVERYONE. *Birthday Club!*

>   *(Everyone freezes in a celebratory pose.)*

>   *(Blackout.)*

End of Play

PROPS & COSTUMES

Onstage Furniture:
1 couch
2 easy chairs
1 coffee table
1 dining table
4 to 6 dining table chairs
1 bar
2 bar stools (optional)
pills

ACT ONE

PROPS

on coffee table:
1 Martini shaker
magazines
1 bowl of crackers
napkins
5 coasters

on dining table:
1 fake birthday cake with unlit candles

on bar:
1 crystal vodka bottle with glass stopper – filled (preferably with water)
napkins
2 regular glasses (for Sarah's orange water)
1 empty wine glass
1 bottle of wine

behind bar:
water (for Sarah)

Scene One:
4 wine glasses with wine – (for Emily, Kathy, Cheryl, and Abbie)
1 fake pregnant belly – Kathy wears
1 makeup brush – Kathy brings in
orange flavoring – Sarah brings in
1 cell phone – Cheryl brings in
1 bottle with pills – Cheryl brings in

Scene Two:
4 wine glasses with wine – (for Emily, Kathy, Cheryl, and Abbie)
1 glass with orange water on coffee table – Kathy hands to Sarah
1 magazine – for Cheryl on coffee table

Scene Three:

4 wine glasses with wine – (for Emily, Kathy, Cheryl, and Abbie)

1 bulge under sweater – Kathy brings in to replace pregnant belly

1 empty coffee cup on coffee table – Kathy spits in it

1 orange water in glass – (for Sarah)

1 cell phone – Abbie brings in

1 cell phone – Kathy brings in

1 cell phone – Cheryl brings in

1 dollar bill – Kathy brings in

ACT TWO

Scene One:

cell phone – Emily brings in

cell phone – Kathy brings in

Scene Two:

4 wine glasses with wine – (for Emily, Kathy, Cheryl, and Abbie)

cell phone – Abbie brings in

cell phone – Kathy brings in

cell phone – Cheryl brings in

Scene Three:

1 wine glass with wine – (for Cheryl)

3 empty wine glasses – on bar

bottle of wine – on bar

empty glass – on the bar

cell phone – Kathy brings in

cell phone – Abbie brings in

cell phone – Emily brings in

orthopedic body brace contraption (Heemish bra) – Sarah brings in

COSTUMES

– There will be four quick changes, Act One, before Scenes Two and Three, and Act Two, before Scenes Two and Three.

– There will be five different costumes for the six scenes. Act One, Scene Three and Act Two, Scene One are the same costumes.

– Sarah's costumes are in the "Heemish" conservative style, and in the last scene she wears the "Heemish bra" under her shirt.

– Cheryl, Emily, Abbie, and Kathy's costumes should be casual clothing that reflects their characters.

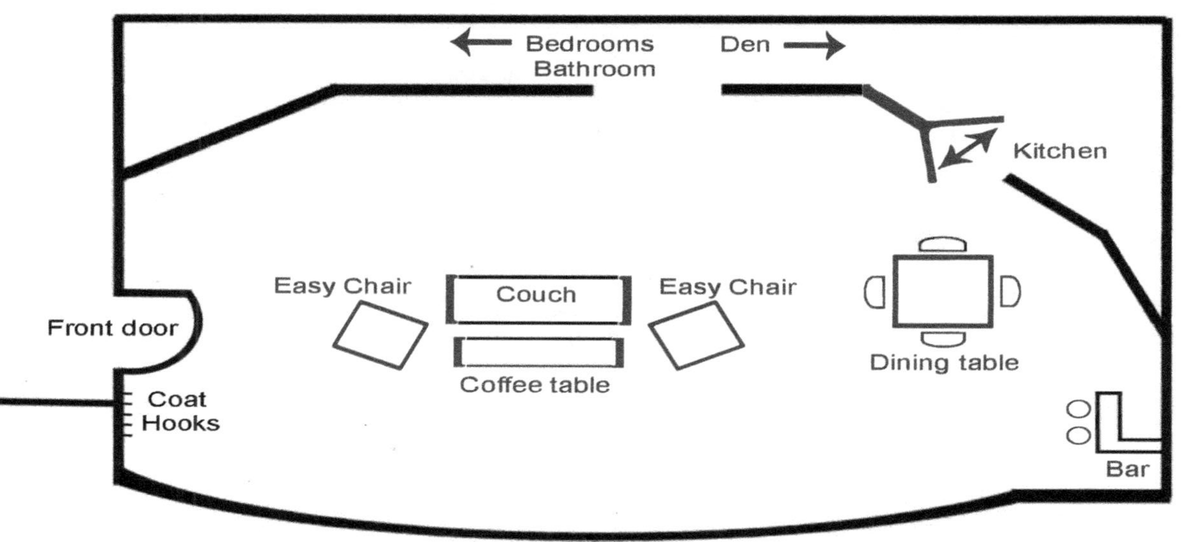

Birthday Club Set Design

www.ingramcontent.com/pod-product-compliance
Lightning Source LLC
Chambersburg PA
CBHW070343120726
47909CB00008B/2733